INTENSITY

C.C. KOEN

INTENSITY Copyright © 2014 C.C. KOEN

PUBLISHED BY: C.C. KOEN
http://www.cckoen.com
Formatting: Polgarus Studio
Cover design: E-book Cover Designs by Carey
Editing: Laurie Boris

This is a work of fiction. Names, characters, places, and events are the product of the author's imagination or used fictitiously. Any resemblance to actual persons, living or dead, business establishments, events, or locales, is entirely coincidental.

The author acknowledges the trademark status and trademark ownership of all trademarks, service marks, and word marks mentioned in this book.

Contains mature content and language. Not recommended for readers under the age of eighteen due to sexual situations and subject matter.

Dedications

This one's for you, Mom.
I miss you every single day.
I felt your love shining down on me as I wrote this story—
my first romance novel.
You always loved them, just like I do.

My one and only baby (even though you're a woman).
Always pursue your dreams.
Don't let anyone or anything stand in the way of you
achieving them.
Remember how much I love you…
To the moon and back, to the moon…

To the readers and anyone that may be…stuck in the past.
I hope you enjoy this story. It's one that's near and dear to my
heart. As the novel evolved it became a story that spoke to me
personally. Thank you for taking time to read it.
I hope you fall in love like I did.

Chapter One

The flawless-skinned woman sitting across the table had to be out of her mind. Maybe I heard her wrong. No, her unsmiling lips and unblinking olive-brown eyes revealed she'd been serious.

I examined the Cafe Haus to see if anyone had overheard her. The loud rock music must have kept her voice from carrying. In the back corner, a girl with punk rocker multi-colored hair, her nose buried in a book, bobbed her head to some tune playing in her earbuds. The only other customer was a gray-haired man on the opposite side, pencil in hand, scribbling in a newspaper.

The coast clear, I leaned across the table toward Mylaynee Johanson and whispered, "You want *me* to be an escort?" I stood with such force my chair skidded across the tile floor, making an eerie screeching noise.

She grabbed my arm. "Please, give me a few minutes to explain."

Embarrassed by the scene the exchange must have created, I scanned the room. The older man gone and the young girl halfway out the back door, I returned my attention to the stranger who'd just rocked my world, as if I needed any more surprises in my life.

Curious, but reluctant, I plunked down in the wooden chair. The previous day while working at a fundraiser, as I shuffled between two crammed tables carrying a tray stacked with overflowing plates, her chair rammed into my leg. Her quick hands and my knee-jerk save kept the other high-profile attendees from wearing their next meal.

Near the end of the evening, she approached me and struck up a chatty conversation. One thing led to another, and before I knew it I disclosed my hectic lifestyle, including three under minimum-wage jobs. When she mentioned a high-paying prospect, the possibility of earning a livable wage had me interested right away. Information exchanged, we agreed to get together. After hearing what she had to offer, it seemed fate got the last laugh, knocking me down another peg and reminding me I had no control or say about the obstacles thrown my way.

Wearing an air of confidence and a white silk pantsuit that no doubt cost more than I made in months, she took a slow sip of her chamomile tea. Her eyes never wavering from mine, she alleged, "It's not a common escort service. You're not forced to sleep with anyone."

What? I cleared my throat. "I don't understand." Scooting my chair closer to the table, I clenched my hands on top and inquired, "How does anyone make money?"

"Sometimes clients need a companion for an event like last night. That's why I was there. It doesn't always include sex." Mylaynee spoke softly and measured as if every word had been

2

well rehearsed. "Background and financials are checked in advance. They're wealthy professionals that pay one- to five-thousand for each date."

Thousand? One particular point kept replaying in my mind, and I spit it out as fast as I thought it. "No sex? I'm guessing there wouldn't be many of those. If you don't get appointments, you don't get paid, right?"

She stirred her tea and spoke to me like we were longtime friends. "You get to choose. It's all agreed to in advance and based on your preferences. If a client wants sex, he's matched with someone who'll provide it. There's a lounge to get to know each other better. It's in a secure building and invitation only. Our apartments are there too, but they aren't permitted in them. It's a strict rule."

"You *live* there?"

"Our boss owns the place and rents to us, but you don't have to. It's convenient and affordable though."

Images of a dilapidated shack with peeling paint and holes in the walls filled my head. A glance down at my clenched hands revealed a crumpled Goodwill linen skirt that had been wrinkle-free this morning. On a debt-laden budget, the store had become a saving grace. This discussion and the lavender-scented perfume she wore made my stomach flip-flop. My silence must not have fazed her, because she continued to reveal more.

"The owner makes sure we're safe, and he manages everything. I've worked there five years and never had a problem. We'd take good care of you, Serena."

My eyes closed, and I drew in a deep breath. The blackness left me in the dark. No insights. No clues. No idea why I was still sitting here. Was this what my life had come to?

Three years ago when Gram was diagnosed with cancer the roller coaster started. As her health continued to decline, I quit college and stayed at her side. She became my priority. After a hard-fought battle, she succumbed to the slow, ravaging disease, leaving me alone and on my own.

I never would've imagined that at twenty-one, I'd be a hundred thousand dollars in debt. Costs for treatments and in-home nursing care, loans, and other money problems I never told Gram about left my finances a mess. One day a week working as a nanny and whatever time I could put into Gram's accounting business wasn't enough to keep up with the bills. After her death, I got the catering job, which brought me to this particular offer.

"Serena." Mylaynee's gentle voice beckoned me.

When I opened my eyes, she reached across the table and rested her hand on my fist. "We can help you," she said with compassion.

"I'm a virgin." The blurted truth seemed to echo in the space. A piece of paper tossed around on the sidewalk all of a sudden became the most fascinating thing in the world. "I don't think I'm qualified."

She squeezed my hand. "No one would know unless you told them. Experience isn't required. Believe me, you'd do very well. I've seen you working a few events in the city. Men can't take their eyes off you. Besides, they'd get off knowing you're a virgin and pay a fortune for the honor."

Yeah, and I'd be surprised if I didn't have an ulcer at the end of this conversation. The blackening storm clouds swirling outside mirrored my tumultuous mood. "I don't think I can do it. Even if the money's as good as you say."

"You don't have to decide right now. Think about it over the weekend. Give me a call on Monday and let me know either way. I'll need more information if you decide to interview. Linc, the owner, handles that." She stood up, a twinkling diamond purse strap slung over her shoulder. "You can do this."

Right, she probably told everyone that.

She strolled out the door carefree like she hadn't just burst the biggest bubble of hope I had building in me since yesterday. As I watched Mylaynee walk away, "The Voice Within" by Christina Aguilera played in the coffee shop. The lyrics struck me and replayed in my head the entire walk back to my apartment, in the pouring rain.

I didn't feel one drop.

Chapter Two

I set the flowers on the roof of my car. My destination framed by two large oak trees at the top of the hill. Sprigs of budding leaves spread along the branches, alerting to the impending season. A few weeks before spring, the weather could be unpredictable, ranging from sunshine, rain, or an occasional lingering snowflake. Overcast with a slight chill in the air, a sudden gust slapped against my face, causing my eyes to water. A loud screeching bird soared overhead. Its large wings flapped against the lofty winds and circled above me multiple times, as if searching for something.

It wasn't the only one.

A glance to the hilltop and another blustery gust sent chills through my bones, numbing my fingertips. I pulled my cardigan closed, knotting the dangling belt around my waist. Flowers in hand and one foot in front of the other, I climbed toward the top, reading each name along the way: Johnson, Finnegan, Langley, Wright, and Smith. At the crest...Thomas.

Kneeling before the headstone, I sat back on my legs. Every Sunday I visited, a time to remember the greatest, most loving person I knew. Her high school portrait, a black-and-white image molded into the marble, reminded me of her constant smile and beautiful features. Our only likeness and my favorite, her sea-green eyes.

"Hi, Gram." Memories of sitting together on the front porch drinking sweet tea and chit-chatting tugged at my heart. "I've been working real hard, but things aren't goin' so well. I know what you'd say. 'No problem is too big. You can do anything you put your mind to.'"

The creaking tree limbs and whistling wind sent another chill through me. I grabbed the collar of my sweater and tucked one flap tighter over the other, dipping my chin to ward off the cold as best I could.

"I'm sorry, Gram. The bank took the house. I tried, but…"

Overwhelmed by my situation, I pressed my temple along the frigid marble surface and sobbed. Tears flowed down my cheeks and chin, pooling in the dirt below.

Help me, Gram. I don't know what to do.

I leaned back and dropped my hands in the dirt. My fingers scrunched into the cold ground, lifting clumps in each hand. I stared as it sifted through my fingers, remembering her last day.

Weak and frail, bedridden for months, she slept most of the time. On occasion she'd wake and mumble, sometimes decipherable, other times not. While I sat at her side, she opened her eyes and called out, "Come here, child."

I rose and leaned closer, smoothing my hands over her thinned hair. She set her fragile hand on my cheek. "Serena, my love, my sweet, sweet girl." Her breath wheezed with each word. "Always remember…good times." Her hand dropped, and I grabbed it, pressing it to my cheek. Her eyes were distant and unfocused as the whistle in her lungs grew louder, the words choppy as she drew in shallow breaths. "Don't be…sad, spread the sunshine, child. Be happy…proud a you…no matter what." She sucked in one quick breath. "Love you." The wheezing slowed and her eyes drifted closed. Never to open again.

I glanced at her headstone and the smiling photo again. "Would you be proud?"

No answer.

A spunky, modern woman, she talked to me about the birds and bees more than once. Encouraged me to date when I turned sixteen. Being a little awkward and shy, it wasn't easy to talk to cute boys in school. When you were one of several hundred and boys had other options like cheerleaders, majorettes, and tons of gorgeous girls, the quiet girl didn't get noticed. My nose constantly buried in schoolbooks or romance novels, I became the wallflower and blended into non-existence. Then Gram got sick, and boys didn't seem so important.

Our lives a whirlwind for as long as I could remember, we were either volunteering or working. When I turned thirteen, the Millers, who lived in our neighborhood, hired me as their nanny one day a week. At sixteen, Gram taught me how to manage her bookkeeping business. She kept up with it, until she couldn't anymore. Most of the larger clients left for more experienced providers when I took over. At eighteen, Gram insisted I continue with my college plans, even though we weren't sure how her illness would progress. I enrolled in an accounting program and took classes until junior year. One day, I'd get that degree.

What should I do, Gram? Give me a sign. Something, anything.

My eyes closed, and I tried to concentrate. To listen.

After some time passed, the quiet became deafening. The sky darkened and millions of stars twinkled overhead. I followed a moonlit path to my car. An imminent decision weighed heavy on my heart, making each step more dismal than the last.

The driver's door open and one foot inside, I looked up the hill. Streams of moonlight beamed down on her headstone like a spotlight, shielding the others in complete darkness. The unusual occurrence sent shivers through me. My hand clenched my anxious stomach while the other pressed on my rapid heartbeat. I made a wish, hoping it reached the great beyond and brought me a resolution.

On the way home, my thoughts flashed from one childhood memory to another. Thankful for Gram's positive outlook, because it took over and provided a temporary reprieve from my uncertain future.

Chapter Three

I got out of my old Toyota and looked around. Noon in Crestfallen and there wasn't one person outside. As I crossed the parking lot, I smoothed my hands along my dress and examined the brick structure that resembled any other apartment building. Five or six stories high, the balconies and large windows at each level would let in tons of natural light. Port Chester Bay flowed behind it, making the sight quite picturesque. Separated by a bridge, the neighborhood encompassed a five-block radius with a handful of small stores and older residences. Most young couples preferred the fast-paced city lifestyle, leaving this area isolated and populated by senior citizens desiring a quieter environment.

About forty minutes north of New York City, it had to be the perfect place for a covert business. No one would ever suspect an escort operation in this tiny town. I grew up not far from here, and it certainly surprised me.

At the front of the building, I pressed the up button on the elevator. My distorted reflection on the metal doors as I shifted from one foot to another reminded me of a fun-house mirror, making me look hideous.

Ugh. Maybe I should've worn a different dress?

The white crochet pattern had a skin-tone shell underneath that matched mine and made it look see-through. But who wore crochet anymore? The mid-thigh length wasn't bad and showcased my bare legs. Under normal circumstances it would be an outfit I'd like very much, but seeing my misshapen image had my stomach twisting into knots. *Okay, don't stress. Think positive.* A self-conscious attitude would not fare well in this interview.

What did I have that could get me the job?

My green eyes, and favorite feature since they were like Gram's, might be appealing. Coppery, pin-straight hair that came down to my hips could be a plus. Men liked long hair, right?

At five foot eleven, the six-inch red stilettos made my legs look amazing. But the extra height made me an Amazon, and ranked as my *least* favorite feature. Normally, I wouldn't choose shoes this high, but I figured women in this profession wore them. At least the erotic books I read claimed so.

If you placed me next to Mylaynee, her exotic beauty with cocoa cream complexion and curvaceous figure would win a man's attention every time, hands down. Last week at the fundraiser, the hunk that accompanied her with blond, spiked-hair in an Armani suit would be just the type to seek her out. No way I'd end up with a gorgeous man like him. With my luck, I'd get stuck with eighty, paunchy, and bald.

The elevator doors slid open to reveal a mirrored interior. Once again all my physical imperfections were on display, combined with gigantic insecurities, and played on my already twisted mind. Before I could move, a panic attack hit me. *Not now.*

Open mouth, breathe in and exhale.

Repeat, deep breath.

The elevator doors started to close, and I flung my hand out, opening them again.

I could do this.

One last deep breath and fingers crossed, I stepped inside. My forehead pressed to the cool mirrored surface, I thumbed the number panel for the top floor, closed my eyes, and gave myself a pep talk.

Pros and cons weighed, the decision to come here marked a time of change. The bank's foreclosing on Gram's house had been the last straw. Everything I'd tried so far hadn't made a bit of difference. Besides, this would be temporary. Mylaynee said I had a choice, so I'd ask for "date-type" as long as I could. Even if I got one a week, I'd still net more than my other paychecks combined. I'd keep the nanny job and continue with bookkeeping, making every little bit count.

I'll get our house back, Gram, I promise.

The doors opened and so did my determined eyes.

Time to put my big girl pants on.

Standing tall and wiping my sweaty palms on my dress, I forced my head up high and took two steps onto the wood floor.

Across the room, a leather sofa with cushions that looked like clouds, comfy enough to sleep on but black like a midnight storm, stretched beneath a huge painting of a nude woman. Abstract ghostly images peered at her sprawled body lying on a settee. One of her hands dangled to the side, palm up, as if panhandling. The other flowed across her brow, a look of exasperation or pleasure I wasn't sure. Her head tilted in my direction welcomed the newcomer and all who graced this domain. Intimate parts exposed, the beautiful figure captivated and mesmerized.

I turned toward the frameless picture windows lining the entire exterior wall and was presented with a breathtaking, unobstructed view of the harbor. Smack dab in the middle, behind an antique mahogany desk, stood the tallest, most impressive man I'd ever seen. The black suit he wore matched the surroundings, professional and sleek. The top three buttons on his white shirt undone, dark sprigs of hair peeked through and begged for my attention.

As I got closer, his eyes scanned me from head, to chest, to hips and up and down my long legs at least three times, resting on my ruby-red tiptoes.

Ha! Two could play at that game. Using the exact pace he did, I snapped mental pictures of every God given, Mr. Universe muscle. A wavy black ponytail, pulled tight at the nape, crested his wide shoulders and dipped to mid-chest, bringing my journey to a momentary pause. A taut dress shirt molded to his pecs became an instant favorite and preference I didn't know I had. As I gravitated lower, the desk impeded my view, coming to rest at his waist and a nondescript silver belt buckle. My eyes drifted back up, wishing I could see more, but his tailored jacket without a hint of lint on it kept him hidden. Still, from what I could take in, the man had sin engraved all over him.

I stopped in front of his desk and realized my earlier assessment of him had been right. My six five in heels, shrunk to five feet the way he towered over me by several inches. "Linc?" The wispiness of my voice made me cringe. Way to go, Serena.

His answer, one sharp nod. In the corners around each eye, little wrinkles appeared as he took another long journey over my body. Knees locked together, I tried hard not to fidget. "I'm Serena. Mylaynee said my interview was at twelve thirty. I'm a little early. I didn't mean to interrupt if you were in the middle of something." Damn, there I went, rambling. Yeah, that would have him eating out of my hands.

Linc rounded the desk, coming toe to toe.

"You're a virgin."

"W-w-what?"

Had Mylaynee told him?

No, she said she wouldn't. It must be my outfit. Stupid! I should've bought the sexy, red dress. Then he *never* would have thought that.

He waited, I guess for a response.

I gathered my courage and stood a little taller. "Is that a *problem*?" I narrowed my eyes, mimicking my best authoritarian schoolteacher glare.

"Have a seat." I could've sworn his reply came out a sigh, when he motioned with a flick of his hand toward the couch.

I stalled, hoping he'd think I could handle alpha males and a little miffed at the way he greeted me. Both of us stared at one another. He squinted, and I noticed his eyes were a shade of blue that reminded me of the cornflower color I used yesterday, drawing spring flowers with the Millers' children.

The longer he looked at me, the more my stomach fluttered, like a thousand birds trying to escape captivity. I sucked in a deep breath and exhaled, shaking the feeling off. My gaze shifted to the comfy looking couch, and I tried to get my head on straight. I really shouldn't piss this man off or he might not hire me. One step taken then another, I concentrated on the woman's image above the sofa. Her hand extended, inviting me to join her.

Evita. That's what I'd name her.

As soon as I sat down, my hands coasted across the soft leather. Just like I'd imagined a cloud would feel. When I looked up, Linc stood in the same place. The blackness of his suit reminded me of a panther's coat, and the man—observing his meal.

He crossed the room and sat next to me, the cushion sinking with his weight and tilting me closer to him. His left leg lined with mine, thigh to heel. He extended an arm along the top of the couch and laid his fingertips on the crease of my neck, brushing them up and down.

Millions of tingles raced over my spine.

His other warm hand took possession of my upper thigh, and he skimmed his thumb back and forth across my clenched legs, creeping upward.

As my dress moved higher and into no man's land, I gripped his wrist and squeezed hard. His fingers stilled at the edge of my panties, making me clench, and the movement on my neck ceased mid-stroke.

"W-what are you doing?"

His pupils transformed to pin pricks and those blue eyes with streaks of jungle green roamed my face in slow motion, as if recording each second to be replayed later.

Never having been this close to a man, I didn't hesitate to examine his intriguing features. His face was stunning, but not perfect. A long and slightly crooked nose might've been broken a time or two. The contrast and part that stole my attention though, his high cheekbones framing succulent red lips that blew slow, even breaths and flowed over my face, heating me all over. His chiseled chin and jaw, which enhanced an already striking face, added to his magnetism. The cologne he wore, or maybe his natural scent, reminded me of woods after a refreshing spring rain blended with a few drops of a fruity, citrus aroma. Bold, yet sweet.

I snapped out of my exploration as soon as his deep voice called out.

"What are you doing here, Serena?"

Chapter Four

Huh? Was that a trick question?

"I-I'm here for a job…as an escort." My brows scrunched together as I tried to figure out what else he might want me to say.

He moved closer, our noses almost touching.

Was he testing me? Trying to see how I might react to domineering, powerful men?

My back stiffened and my grip on his hand tightened, squeezing it to death. His pulse beat rapidly on my fingertips. He dropped his head, almost clipping me in the nose, and sucked in a deep, ragged breath as if he needed to get control.

His silence disturbed me, so I spit out the first thing that came to mind. "Mylaynee said the interview was a—" but I didn't get to finish, as he bolted up from the couch and stared me down. Whatever I wanted to say vanished, and his serious face made me crush the cushion in my fists and sit ramrod straight.

"Why are you here?" His clipped words, exasperated and peeved.

I closed my eyes, scrunching them tight. I didn't want to tell him about my situation. I just needed the damn job!

"Please." My whisper so low, I barely heard it in my own ears. I opened my eyes and from my seated position begged. "I need a job...that pays well, pays a lot, *this job*." My voice grew stronger with each plea.

Quiet for what seemed like an eternity, his gaze never left mine. He shook his head, and announced matter-of-factly. "You'll be exclusive."

"What does that—"

He yanked me up from my seat and launched his lips on mine so fast the contact zapped me with a thousand volts. His strokes, bold at first, lightened to soft, tender kisses almost as if he was asking permission to enter—to taste.

The heat from his hands, holding my upper arms, seared me.

My fists clenched and unclenched over and over at my sides.

Touch him? Don't touch him?

Unable to deny myself, I moved closer, aligning my body with his. My hands gravitated of their own volition, melting to his tight abs and drifting upward, over his chest and up to his neck, where I held on for the ride.

His loud groan rumbled across my breasts, and his firm arms wound around my back, crushing me against him.

For the first time in my life, I surrendered and parted my lips, ready to welcome him in. Instead of tongues diving toward one another, Linc stilled and clamped his mouth shut. As I started to step away, he clenched my hips, holding me in place. He pressed his forehead to mine and slammed his eyes closed.

Kiss me, please.

"Serena," he whispered against my mouth. The tip of his tongue sliding along my bottom lip in a sensual, taunting tease.

So, so good, yet so darn bad.

My hold on his neck tightened as I tried not to rub myself against him, but my body had a mind of its own.

His hand drifted up my neck and through my hair; the other gripped the small of my back, melding us chest, hips, and thighs. He slipped his tongue in and circled mine, first clockwise then counterclockwise and back again, lingering and savoring for a long while.

Mmm…peppermint. My new favorite flavor.

Clasped in his tight embrace, I could feel our hearts beating in rhythm with one another. After what seemed like an eternity he took a languid step back, bringing my first kiss to an end. Biting the corner of my lip, I could taste his sweetness on me.

He set his fingertips on my temple and skimmed downward, across my cheek and to my chin, as if memorizing a map. His tender, reverent touch had my heart and breath seizing. He slid a thumb in a tender swipe across my lower lip, following it with a flash of a crooked smile. The euphoria of the moment almost made me grin too, but I couldn't move in my state of shock and awe.

"Beautiful," he breathed down on me, coating my body in a wave of foreign emotions. As quick as he made the pronouncement, he dashed away to a bar in the far corner. The brief encounter went from a hundred passionate degrees to frigid in a second.

What just happened?

Stuck in the spot he left me, my nerves launched to jumping jacks in the pit of my stomach. He fixed a drink and didn't bother to look at me again. I opened my mouth to speak, but my tongue seemed superglued, making it impossible to utter a word.

"The apartments are one or two bedrooms. I have both available. Mylaynee can show you hers. That way you'll know what to expect. They're not furnished, get a mover or I'll have my men do it. Since you're exclusive, you'll live here rent-free," Linc recited in a calm and professional manner; our momentary kiss fest hadn't seemed to have impacted him in the least.

Unfazed by my wordless mouth, opening and closing multiple times, he continued. "You're to be available every night from six till the next morning. Sunday is everybody's day off. What you're wearing won't do. Go to Forté and tell Liza I sent you. She'll bill my account. Take Mylaynee with you, she knows what you need."

His large hand extended to me from behind the bar. "Take this."

"I don't drink." My brain and mouth kicked into gear at his demanding tone.

"A toast, to your new job."

I walked over and took the tumbler, examining the contents. "What is it?"

He smiled wide, cocking his brow. "Fifty-year-old scotch," he stated, clinking his glass with mine.

I nodded and chugged it with a coughing after-effect.

He chuckled, saluted me, and downed his too. "You'll bartend starting tonight. Be in the lounge ready to prep by six. Doors open at seven. Your prior experience should help, but I'll have someone train you anyway. When you're able to handle it solo, let me know. I prefer two serving, but I'll schedule three until you're ready."

"Where's the lounge?"

He thumbed backward toward double mahogany doors.

"You'll be paid a thousand a week. Tips are generous, so add another thousand. You don't report them to me, they're yours." Filling the glass to the brim, he took a fortifying gulp. The light blue in his eyes clouded over and a rumbling black swirl of cyclone proportions appeared. "I want to make something very clear, Serena…" He stretched across the bar, stopping an inch from my nose. "When you're done each night, you come to me. *My* bed, no one else's. Is that clear?"

Oh my God.

I couldn't speak, even if I'd wanted to. My chin dropped down and when I scraped it back up off the floor, it snapped shut so fast, my tongue vibrated along every nerve.

A knock at the door interrupted the silence.

When he opened it, Mylaynee's gaze darted to me and back to him. "I'm sorry, did I interrupt?"

The doorway shrunk to miniature as his enormous physique and sensual energy consumed the opening, bridging

21

the distance. "Giving her the lay of the land: lounge, apartment, shopping."

"I can help with that."

Full attention back on me, he said, "When you get back, come to the lounge and meet up with B.B. She'll train you tonight."

"You ready to go?" Mylaynee urged, excitement bouncing from her to me.

"Sure." At the door, Linc's stretched, fixed position had my chest brushing his. One of the crochet loops hooked onto his shirt button, snapping me back a step. My surprised breath caught a whiff of his intoxicating cologne, the taste stinging my tongue and reminding me of our passionate kiss. I pressed two fingers on my lips, trying to get the tingles to stop and numbness to go away.

A warm palm cupped my cheek. Linc ducked down to my height, holding me in his gaze. The earlier storm dissolved before my eyes, replaced by a youthful luminance. A dimple appeared above the crease of his lip, like a glimmering star positioned northeast, guiding weary wanderers in a new direction.

He used the pad of his thumb to outline my lips, tracing the ridge, into the dip, then back down, trailing across the bottom and stopping where my fingers had been.

My face heated, and went from blushing to red hot as I ducked and scurried into the hallway, ending up next to a beaming Mylaynee.

"Show her your place then take her to Forté." He shot another glance my way, but didn't say anything. Instead his prodding chin signaled, *get going*.

Mylaynee guided me into an adjoining vacant room just like any other New York City high-end lounge. Around the perimeter, plush cushioned high back chairs situated at round mirror-top tables and a vintage bar with pearlescent inlays framing a mahogany base completed the furnishings. Behind it, three shelves lined the wall from one end to the other and were stocked full of a wide assortment of liquors, some in glass vaults with key locks. Wow, I'd never seen that before. At least thirty on the top shelf, it had to be very expensive to keep that secure.

"You ready? We're going that way." She pointed toward an exit on the left, and I followed her like an imprinting duckling, tracking each step. I crossed my fingers, hoping she'd take me under her wing and help me find my way through unfamiliar territory.

She turned around, linked her arm through mine, and offered an encouraging smile, making me believe she would.

Chapter Five

Mylaynee showed me around her place, an open space concept quadruple the size of my soon to be former apartment. The living areas had tons of natural light pouring in through wall-to-wall sliding glass doors. Out on the balcony, the stunning scenery included a beautiful bay with motorboats and fishing trawlers. I crossed my fingers once again, wishing for the same view.

Back inside, she motioned me to a stool and entered a kitchen decked out with stainless steel appliances, granite counter tops, and cherry wood cabinets. She pulled a jug of tea from the fridge and shook it. "You want some?"

"Sure." I scanned the living and dining areas. The terra cotta walls and walnut wainscoting made the room warm and homey. Masks with various expressions in a rainbow of colors accented one spot. Two sofas in the living room and the dinette chairs had woven, geometric patterned upholstery. Tables constructed of holey driftwood with dark and light striations gave it a naturalistic vibe. A style Mother Earth would be proud of and might reveal a little about her ethnicity. Her darker complexion, high-angled cheeks, and slim oval eyes resembled Asian or Native American heritage. The overall combination and her classy clothes must drive men crazy.

Before she turned around and gave me one of the full glasses, I realized I'd been staring. To play it off, I looked outside, appreciating the way the sunshine brightened the room. "You have a nice place."

"Thanks. If you need any help let me know. I love decorating." She extended a glass to me, while taking a sip from hers. "The interview went well?"

Not wanting to reveal too many personal details, I displayed my best poker face. "Linc said I'd be exclusive. Is that something he does with new escorts?"

Her brows scrunched, and she set her drink on the counter. "*Exclusive?* H-he told you that?"

Crap. Was it code for something illicit in this business? I gripped the counter, bracing for the worst and nodded.

She dashed around the half wall and sat next to me with wide eyes. "Since I've been here that's never happened." She grabbed my arm and shook it. "Clients can arrange to be with one woman for a specified time, if she agrees."

I fell back in my seat. "I don't understand. He said I'm to come to his bed and no one else's."

She stared at me. "Hot damn, girl! That means you're exclusive to *him*." Her hand on my arm tightened, and she shook me again, this time almost knocking me off the stool.

"But…look at me." I waved my hand up and down my body. Why would he choose me over the other women?

"I told you when we met. You got *it,* girl." She shrugged one shoulder. "You're hired and have something no one else does. So don't worry about it. Besides, Linc's a nice guy. He'll take good care of you."

Adele's "Rumour Has It" played from somewhere in the room. Mylaynee answered the call. A few seconds later she returned to my side. "We need to get to Forté. I'll drive."

From what I'd heard about the store, celebrities jetted there to purchase casual, business, or evening wear. They had on-site seamstresses and tailors catering to every whim. Custom-made clothing designed from scratch within a forty-eight hour period guaranteed.

Yesterday Goodwill, today Forté. Amazing how fast a person's life could change with one decision.

☙

Mylaynee rushed into the store like she owned the place. A woman, about two feet shorter than me with gray hair and wearing a dark blue suit approached us with a huge grin and engulfed her in a hug.

"Mylaynee, my favorite customer, it's good to see you, dear. I have those new designs you ordered in the back, I'll get them for you."

"Liza, this is Serena." Mylaynee turned toward me and nudged me forward. "Linc sent her. You get to spoil her rotten."

I extended my hand, but the small woman surprised me when she hugged me too. Tears sprung to my eyes at the welcoming embrace. Her height and tender smile reminded me of Gram. God, I missed her so much. Before Liza released me, I wiped the corner of my eye, hoping neither woman saw the emotion on my face.

She pulled back and observed me head to toe. "You're gorgeous. I have so many dresses that will look wonderful on your tall frame. Have you done any modeling?"

"No, my gram's friends used to tell me I should, but…" My voice drifted off and I looked away, memories choking me once again.

She grasped my hand, holding it tight. "Let's get you in the back and have the girls make a fuss over you. They like that." She laughed and pulled me along. I glanced at Mylaynee, trailing behind me with a huge grin on her face.

"Smile," she mouthed.

When I turned back around, we had entered a large room with gold couches on the left and right. In the center sat a raised round platform and behind it a mirror that extended from ceiling to floor.

Good grief.

Mylaynee plopped down on a sofa, stretching her legs in front of her like she planned to be here a while.

Great, just great.

A lady with a clipboard in hand pressed a buzzer and within seconds another woman brought out drinks and finger foods on a silver cart.

You've got to be freaking kidding me. Ugh! This was all too much.

Two women entered the room. Both looked younger than me, dressed in gold silk tops and black pants. They could be twins and wore similar, professional expressions that said,

"Let's do this." Moments later with arms full of clothes, they rushed off to a room behind Mylaynee. I watched it all unfold like the movie, *Pretty Woman*. Ready to pinch myself to make sure I hadn't been magically transported to the set.

A loud clap broke me out of my trance. "Okay everyone. This is Serena. Lincoln sent her to us. She gets a complete wardrobe. Tricia and Katrina, keep the clothes coming including undergarments, shoes, everything."

The twins nodded.

"I'll help her get dressed. The rest of you know what to do."

They all smiled.

Liza ushered me into a gold-draped dressing room with a couch and dresses galore hanging everywhere. An antique mirror positioned in the corner and classical music filled the small space—tranquil and regal at the same time.

"Serena," Liza's voice jolted me. "This may seem a little overwhelming, but we'll take good care of you." She squeezed my arm. "Have fun, enjoy it. It's nice to get all dolled up." Her sweet smile made my heart pinch, but I returned the gesture.

"Thank you, for everything," I whispered.

"It'll be okay. You'll see."

Like a hidden message, I could hear Gram's voice as she said those exact words to me the last three years of her precious life. A huge lump formed in my throat.

Goodness, why were these memories hitting me now?

I sucked in a shuddered breath and looked down at my twisting hands, getting control so I didn't make an idiot of myself in front of complete strangers.

A dark green dress shimmered in front of me. Thick wide straps darted to a sweetheart neckline. A thin, diamond chain hung around the middle. The length might sit a little above the knee, but I couldn't tell for sure until I put it on. It looked…modest.

Huh, maybe this wouldn't be so bad after all.

Then Liza flipped it around.

My mouth fell open.

The material scooped way down and would no doubt dip to my ass. I guess I should be grateful that wasn't the front.

"That is the back, right?"

Liza laughed. "It's going to look amazing with your hair and skin color. Just wait and see. Come on, let's get you in it."

I didn't look in the dressing room mirror after we slipped it on. Instead I kept staring at the silvery mesh stilettos, hoping I didn't trip on the way out.

"It fits you perfectly, dear. Go out to the platform and let Maria and Kara take a look. They're the seamstresses and have a great eye. I'm sure they'll agree though."

When I entered the room, all eyes darted my way. A chorus of gasps and sighs could be heard throughout the space. One step onto the platform, and I still hadn't looked in the mirror. *Chicken.*

Mylaynee rushed up to me, clasping my hand in hers. "Damn, girl. That color is stunning on you. I got chills. Imagine what Linc will do when he sees you."

I giggled, and my nerves settled a bit.

Behind me, the seamstresses murmured to each other, tugging and adjusting the fabric.

I winked at Mylaynee. "Thanks."

"On our way home, I'll pick up an oxygen mask and a defibrillator for Linc."

The room swelled with laughter, and the remainder of the afternoon passed by with light-hearted banter as I tried on one outfit after another, complete with shoes and the sexiest lingerie I'd ever seen.

The ladies treated me like a princess.

All the while the little voice in my head countered, "Fool."

Chapter Six

Promptly at six, I entered the lounge. The enormous room must run the entire length of the building. Walls painted the same platinum color as Linc's office gave it a chic vibe. When I got to the bar in the back corner, an interesting feature caught my attention. Rather than a wood top, a crystal cover edged in a crisscross pattern provided an unobstructed view of broken liquor bottles, all different sizes and colors scattered on a mirrored base. An amazing serving area and unlike any I'd seen before, the "L" design had to be near thirty foot long and seemed tiny in this large gathering space.

No one else here yet, I decided to get acclimated with the liquor. My former catering job trained and rotated employees from serving tables to tending bar. That way, if anyone ever called off they'd be covered. Since I preferred serving food, I often chose it when they needed a replacement. Either way, the skills would come in handy.

A voice cleared from behind me. I turned around, and the little bit of confidence I'd stored throughout the day took a nosedive.

"I'm B.B. and this is Fallon," she introduced in a sing-song voice as we shook hands. "You must be Serena, nice to meet you."

"I was taking a look around. I hope you don't mind." Even in the amazing Forté green dress, which accentuated my favorite features, these women made me look like an Oompa Loompa.

"No, it's fine. Let's get started," B.B. said. A classic blonde that could be a modern-day pin-up, she had wavy white-blonde hair that cascaded to her hips. A stark contrast to Fallon standing next to her with auburn locks and a side bang that draped over her left eye. Fallon and I both towered over B.B., who couldn't be more than five foot five in her stilettos.

The hour went by fast as we discussed various routines, cut garnishes, stocked shelves, and cleaned tables. At seven the doors opened and gorgeous women of all shapes and sizes filled the room. Their scantily clothed bodies on full display, delighting the men following close behind. The clients seemed to range in age from mid-twenties to a refined seventy. Most good-looking and well-dressed, typical white-collar type. But if they paid the prices Mylaynee mentioned, they must be higher up on the corporate chain, or whatever income ladder qualified them to be here.

Similar to other company events, people danced and gathered in groups, talking above the rapid beating rock music. Except in this place, hands roamed all over bodies, and PDA didn't happen behind closed doors. Hmm, so sex clubs did exist beyond the pages of a book.

B.B. worked alongside me a while. When I handled each order without making any mistakes, she told me to grab her if I needed help and skirted off to the other end of the bar. The three of us covered the constant orders without delay and worked well together.

Ducked into a bottom cabinet, I reached for a whiskey bottle. At that moment a large hand swept the exposed skin along my spine and gripped me around the neck. I bolted upright and came face to face with Linc.

"Nice dress." His gaze dropped to my lips and lower. He snagged the diamond chain belt and reeled me into him. "How's it going?" His devilish baritone zinged along my nerves. In a lazy caress, he rubbed his thumb on the silk dress, lengthways along my hipbone.

Even in a crowded room consumed with perfume and cologne, his bold scent took hold and I got lost in his shimmering blue eyes. It took me several seconds before I responded with a husky "Fine," but it probably came out a gurgle as saliva pooled in my mouth. Yep, real smooth, Serena.

Taking a step back from him, I bumped into the counter. A comical grin spread across his face. That got my head back in the game and I crooned with sugary sweetness, "Can I get you a drink, *boss*?" I matched his smirk with one of my own. The man intrigued the heck out of me.

"Serena," he said, coughing through a chuckle.

What's so funny?

B.B. bumped her shoulder into mine, butting between us. "Can I get you anything, Linc?" she purred.

Oh, boy. I dashed off and kept myself busy with customers. A while later with a couple minutes of downtime, I surveyed the scene. One of my favorite things to do—people watch.

Several clients tugged and brushed Fallon's bangs from her brow, flashing overconfident smiles. I guess when presented with a sure thing, it increased assurances. Men were so easy. No wonder history had dozens of countries falling at the hands of a woman.

B.B., however, compelled the entire room. Men tracked her every step, as if pulled by a magnetic field. I guess it helped that her dress had a gigantic slit down the front. Every move resulted in an eyeful of her overabundant, double-D breasts.

Dang, she made me look so—blah. *Ugh.*

Mylaynee waved at me from across the room. The blond guy I saw her with at the fundraiser stood at her side again. He stared at me and then whispered in her ear. She shook her head and punched him in the arm. Ha! She smacked him like a brother. Interesting. I'd have to ask her about him sometime.

At least five men hovered around the fifty plus women in attendance. Throughout the evening, clients gave me drink orders but didn't say anything else. Granted I had no clue when it came to men, but I didn't get a lame pick-up line, a flexing muscle, or even a flashing grin. Nada. Not one illicit remark. It wasn't the reaction I expected.

Fallon tapped me on the shoulder, mouthing "break" over the blaring music and pointed toward a hallway. Earlier she'd showed me an adjoining room with several small sofas and tables, and an employee lounge that didn't have loud tunes playing, making it a good place to relax. Dropping into a comfy club chair wide enough for two linebackers, I kicked off a stiletto and propped my foot on a knee, massaging it. *Ah*, the blood began to circulate, but pain lingered and pulsed around my ankle. Not used to wearing heels while serving, the numbness built throughout the night. The little reprieve felt good.

About to switch to the other foot, the door opened and Linc strutted in, glimpsing down at my hands. Hopping up, I lost my balance in only one heel. His firm grasp on my shoulders kept me from falling flat on my face. "Whoa, steady there."

My death grip on his arm increased as I hobbled on one foot. "Sorry," I mumbled, scooping my shoe off the floor and putting it back on.

B.B. stormed in, catching us in an unintentional embrace. She glared at me, announcing, "A client needs you, Linc."

Another smarty-pants grin on his face, he buckled the shoe strap I hadn't noticed was undone and left. Yeah, I made quite the stupid impression for sure. If I wasn't under so much pressure to do a good job, I'd laugh at myself too. My goal had been to get through the night without doing something wrong and Linc firing me. So far the awkward moments, although embarrassing, could be fluffed off. But B.B.'s pinched lips and scowl indicated my semi-optimistic outlook might be taking a turn—for the worst. Hands on her hips she ordered, "Don't take too long. It's busy and we need help." A slamming door followed her on the way out.

Okay.

In the hallway leading back to the bar, I focused on the monstrous heels that only a man would have invented. Out of nowhere, a sweaty hand grabbed my upper arm and dragged me into a dark alcove. I wobbled on my unsure feet as a man launched a full-body press, slamming my back against a cold wall. His heavy panting sent a bitter stench up my nose. *Ew.*

My hands fisted, and I shoved his chest, but his hefty body didn't budge. Fear hit me, twisting my stomach in knots and locking me in place.

"I've been watching you all night, hoping I'd get you alone. We're going to have some fun, *you* and *me*. Right here."

He'd hit two points on a Breathalyzer if tested. Just my luck, the one person to approach me for sex was wasted. I turned my face away, taking a gulp of semi-fresh air and attempted to think of a way out of this. Damn, if I had experience I'd know what to say. *Come on, Serena, think of something.*

"How about we go back to the bar. I'll buy you a drink?" A raspy, sexy response came out as bile rose in my throat. I hoped the fly-by-the-seat-of-your-pants method worked, because I wanted the heck out of this position and ill-fitting nook.

He captured my wrists and twisted, smashing them against the wall. Our bodies sealed together chest to knee. "You want it. I tip *real* well." His hard shaft shoved forward, he rubbed up and down between my clenched thighs.

Oh, gross.

"Get off her. Now." Linc's bellowing growl made me jump.

The inebriated fool paid no attention. He bent his head back and laughed, blowing fumes up my nostrils that could get *me* drunk.

Linc's stranglehold on the guy's barely-there neck unleashed a squeal so high he could've alerted a neighborhood fifty miles away. His hands dropped from mine when Linc hurled him backward, pitching him at least ten feet. His unsteady body hit a wall and smashed face down.

Ouch.

Mesmerized by the crumpled man, I flinched when feather-light fingertips brushed my face from temple to chin and settled on my neck. Transfixed in Linc's searching eyes, I murmured a hollow and head spinning "Hi."

He rubbed my arms, up and down, the warmth lessening shivers I couldn't control. "You okay?" he whispered.

Reality set in and I grabbed his elbows, pulling him against me. My cheek lying on his shoulder, I sucked in a deep breath, inhaling his natural fragrance and calming my heart- pounding nerves. He drew me into a reassuring hug and rocked me in a gentle sway. "You want to go back to my apartment? You could lie down and relax."

I squeezed his waist and looked up at him. "Thank you…for helping me."

He held my face in his hands and announced, "You don't need to worry about him or that happening again. I'll make sure of it."

Comfort needed wherever I could find it, I leaned against him and dropped my forehead to his chin. Thoughts of what could have happened in this dark alcove had me swallowing several times and willing a blood-rushing headache to go away.

His fingers kneaded my shoulders as he murmured, "I promise, no one will bother you again." The sincerity and gentleness in his voice eased some of my anxiety. "Come on, I'll walk you to my apartment." He took a step sideways, but I gripped his arms, stopping him.

The dim space made it difficult to see his concerned face, but I studied it anyway. "I'm not gonna leave the girls short-handed. I'll be okay." To lighten the mood I said with a forced smile, "Besides it's my first night. I don't want to disappoint my boss."

He stroked a thumb across my cheek and examined my better-be-disguised-face. "You sure? It's okay to call it a night."

I shook my head and stood up straighter, determined to show him I could handle this job. "No, thank you though."

He linked our fingers together in a sure and comforting grip, and escorted me back to a jam-packed bar. Two hours from close, I jumped in and put on the performance of my life. My personal, protective shadow never out of sight.

ツ

Flames flickering in the fireplace mesmerized me. A glass of red wine in hand, I twirled it while resting my head along the couch. After an exhausting evening, Linc led me to his apartment. Radiant heat from the fire warmed my feet propped up on the couch, creating a cozy atmosphere and a comfortable place to collapse.

Without much thought given to the drunk or the fact I hadn't seen him again, the evening flew by. The rote method of taking orders, preparing drinks, and serving one person after another kept my mind occupied. Now that I had a chance to think about it, the whole thing happened so fast. A year of self-defense training in high school didn't make a bit of difference. What an idiot. I could have handled it so much better. *I should have laid him flat on his ass.* The number of times I'd done that in class couldn't be counted.

Linc's long fingers enclosed mine and pulled the full glass away. I lifted my groggy gaze as he took a gulp and set it aside. He knelt down in front of me and rested a hand in my lap while the other brushed several strands of hair from my face, tucking it behind my ear.

"You tired?" His peaceful tone had me burrowing into the cushions and staring at his profile. Firelight added to the shadows on his scruffy cheeks, making him even sexier and bringing to life the description: tall, dark, and handsome. In my mind I envisioned coasting my fingers across his jaw followed by my lips. Instead I nodded my reply and crossed my fingers, hoping I'd dream of a knight in shining armor who looked like the sweet man gazing back at me.

In an instant, he swooped me off the couch and nestled me against his broad chest. I dropped my head on his shoulder, wrapped my arms around his neck, and breathed in his intoxicating scent. As he moved, my eyes drifted closed, picturing the two of us in a passionate kiss, embracing…making love.

He set me in the middle of a king-sized bed and his molten blue eyes scanned me head to toe. "Let's get this dress off."

My sleepy, calm breathing vaulted to heavy panting. I watched, mesmerized as he slid the zipper at my ribs downward, baring more and more skin. It took all my might not to stop him. My body in no way compared to the others he saw every day. Even though I jogged and exercised daily, my small, thirty-six B breasts and large hips looked unbalanced with my beanpole height.

As his fingers swept along my skin, pulling the straps down, a thousand sparks jolted my body. When he had the dress off, he threw it to the corner chair like the silk burned his fingers. Then he took a few steps back.

My hands shot up; one covered my constricted nipples and the other spread wide, shielding between my legs. His hooded gaze skimmed the baby blue demi-bra and thong. All my insecurities exposed and on display for him.

He lifted each of my arms, and the longer he inspected them the more his brows scrunched. His thumbs brushed along my inner wrists and his ominous tone spoke volumes. "That bastard *bruised* you."

"Linc—"

My mouth slammed shut when he pressed the gentlest kiss on each wrist and laid them at my side. He pulled a comforter up to my chin and tucked the edges in around me. Another kiss, similar to the one Gram used to place on my temple to say good night, but his somehow said more than that. "Sleep," he whispered in my ear, and again I heard so much more. It had been quite a while since someone took care of me, long before Gram passed. Overwhelmed by a flood of emotions and unable to look away, I forced my overtired eyes to stay open.

Across the room, he stood watchful. His previous anger dissolved, replaced by a concerned but tender expression, causing a thrumming pitter-patter in my tummy and chest.

After the door shut, I rolled over, crossed my fingers, and went to sleep.

Chapter Seven

In the middle of an awesome dream I heard, "Wake up, sleepy head," as one soft kiss after another lingered on my neck. I forced my eyes open and saw Linc's crooked grin inches from my face. "Good morning, beautiful. I made coffee," he greeted with cheer.

Ugh, I hated morning people.

I tried to roll over, but he pointed to the steaming mug sitting on the nightstand.

"What time is it?" I croaked with a raspy pre-coffee voice and burrowed further into the plush pillows. My slow-to-compute brain didn't register much unless I had two or three cups first.

"Six. You have to go to the Millers', little Miss Nanny."

I sprung up and shook my head. "Wait, how'd you know that?"

He crossed his arms and cocked a brow at me. "I'm the boss. I know all."

Why did he have to be so darn cute?

Exhausted, I dropped back down even though I had one of the best night's sleep in a long time. His bed was so comfortable. I didn't want to get out.

All of a sudden the covers were yanked away. What the…?

"Linc!" I tried to snatch the blankets back, but he threw the entire comforter off the bed. "Hey!" I leapt over the side and stood with my hands on my hips.

He winked and walked backward toward the door. "Drink your coffee, Serena. Get going or you'll be late."

The further away he got the more I noticed. He had on black and white track pants, riding low on his hips, and a red tee that emphasized his ripped physique. Man, if I missed *that* sitting right next to me, then I needed caffeine bad.

He caught my thorough inspection and laughed, causing his chest muscles to ripple. "I'm headed out for a run. Help yourself to anything in the kitchen. Make yourself at home." In a repeat of last night, his half-lidded eyes skimmed my body, one inch after another all the way to my toes.

I looked down. Oh, crap. From a nearby chair, I snatched one of his T-shirts and threw it over my head. It fell to mid-thigh and covered my bra and panties.

"Do you need help moving your stuff over here?" He leaned against the door frame casual-like.

I couldn't afford movers so… "Yeah, uh, you mentioned you have some people that could do that, right?"

"I'll give Sal a call and we'll have you moved in before you get back. You want a one or two bedroom?" he asked then snapped his fingers, "Give me the key to your apartment."

Noticing my purse on the nightstand, I removed the key from the clasped ring and tossed it to him. "One bedroom's good."

He stalked toward me like a man on a mission, smoothed the key along my bottom lip, and dragged it to my chin. His eyes softened as he explored mine. "Thanks." He leaned in, rubbing his chest along my already hard nipples. My breath hitched, and the hair on my arms and nape prickled from his touch like static electricity.

He sauntered backward, a huge smile on his face when he left the room. "Have a nice day, beautiful." I glanced up at the ceiling and hugged my shoulders, squeezing tight.

On the way to the bathroom, I downed a much-needed jolt of caffeine.

♈

After a wild day of running after the Millers' three young kids, I pulled into the garage and parked near the elevator. Less than a year after Gram passed, I had *another* new place to live. When Linc said I didn't have to pay rent it was a huge relief. Not having the extra cost each month would reduce my debt much quicker.

Mylaynee's text said my new apartment wasn't far from hers, and she'd have a key for me. Fingers crossed, I hoped for a balcony and water view. I'd sit there with coffee, enjoying the fresh air and serenity of it all.

Last night, I met most of the women. We didn't have much time to talk beyond brief introductions, but they seemed nice. Still, I wondered what it'd be like living here. Until now, I hadn't hung out with too many girls around my age. Gram always toted me along with her friends from one volunteer activity to the next, "spreading the sunshine." The past six months without her had been lonelier than I could've ever imagined. Maybe the void would be filled in some way. I couldn't help but get excited at the possibility of making friends.

Maybe I'd fit in—belong—for a while.

When I got to the third floor, I examined the quiet hallway. I counted four doors on both sides. The slate-blue walls with cherry wood wainscoting made it look classy. Mylaynee stood in her entryway and greeted me dressed in a yellow and orange kimono that was stunning with her dark skin color. "How were the kids today?"

"Don't ask," I grumbled and sat on a stool at the kitchen counter. "They were all over the place. Our first warm day in a while and they went crazy. Thank God I took them to the park. We slid, swung, and anything else their devious little minds could come up with. One thing's for sure, they'll sleep good tonight."

She got two mugs out of the cabinet, mixed apple cider with rum, and popped it in the microwave.

"What're you doing?"

"It's medicinal." She giggled and pointed a spoon at my frowning face. "No arguments, girl. You need this."

"Do you have the key?"

She smiled and grabbed it off the top of the refrigerator, setting it in front of me. At the beep, she stirred and gave me a cup. Casual and graceful, she sat next to me, taking a drink of the spiked concoction.

"Have you been in that apartment?" I inquired, blowing on the steamy liquid before taking a sip. *Darn that's good.* Several gulps later, the warm cider soothed my weary bones.

"It's been empty, so I haven't seen it in a long time, but the layouts are all the same. You can paint or decorate any way you like. Linc doesn't mind if we add personal touches."

I took another swig. "That's nice."

"He's not like other bosses. I've heard horror stories from the girls about other places. He's different and not bad on the eyes." She smirked and butted her shoulder into mine as if we were co-conspirers sharing the same thought.

I cleared my throat. "He's...sweet." My face heated as I remembered the way he tucked me in bed last night and his comical wake-up call.

She sighed and said in a thoughtful voice, "He helped me through a bad time, so yeah, he's a great guy. I'd never want to get on his bad side though. I've witnessed it and wouldn't want to be on the receiving end."

All my warm feelings vanished. "D-do you mean with the women?"

"No," she reassured. "He's all business where that's concerned. With clients though, if any of them get out of line, he's on them."

My gaze drifted to the mug. "Yeah, that kinda happened last night..." Not finishing the story, instead I chugged the rest of the fortifying drink.

"What? I didn't know that." Her voice rose, and she gripped my shoulder.

I gave her a comforting smile, appreciating her concern. "Someone got a little rough and Linc took care of him."

She patted my hand. "Your first night on the job. Geez, girl." She pulled me into a firm hug. "If you ever want to talk about anything come see me, promise?" She pulled back and looked me in the eyes. "I'd like to think we're friends, Serena, so come to me, okay?"

Touched by her kind offer and support, I gave her arm a tender squeeze. "Thanks, and yeah, we're friends. But only because you make *kick-ass* apple cider."

She tipped her mug to mine and then finished drinking it. "Come on." She pulled me off the stool. "Let's go check out your new place."

We walked to apartment three-ten, laughing the entire way.

It came complete with a balcony and a million-dollar view.

The last bag unpacked, I heard three knocks at the door. I swung it open to find Linc dressed in another black suit and a cover model next to him. Poised with one leg extended and hip cocked in a shimmery red dress, she could be strutting down a catwalk at a moment's notice. That must be one heck of a push-up bra she had on, because those babies were bursting through her swoopy neckline.

Doesn't anyone wear turtlenecks anymore?

Linc kissed my temple. "Getting settled?" He smiled and rejoined the Tyra Banks doppelganger, placing his hand on her lower back. "This is Monique. Monique…Serena." I examined the two of them, tens on the sexuality scale, and disliked her in an instant.

Her eyes scanned me, head to toe and back again. I bristled at her blatant perusal, like she couldn't quite figure out why he'd employ someone like me. She extended her hand and said in a bored tone, "Pleasure to meet you."

Yeah, right. I returned the shake and blocked the doorway. "Did you need something?"

I glanced between them and calculated how to get rid of her. Not expecting visitors, I had on thrift store cut-off sweats and a ratty tank top. My "lazy-butt clothes" and my preferred at-home garb.

"Monique's going to look at the apartment."

I grabbed the doorknob, twisting it instead of slamming it in her face. "I don't understand."

He pulled me aside. "She's my designer. You can use her to redecorate."

She strolled in and posed again, this time head and nose in the air, scrutinizing every nook and cranny between the living room and kitchen.

My mouth fell open even further and snapped shut. "I appreciate the offer, but I don't need anything done. It's fine the way it is." I pointed toward the interior so he could see inside— not that he couldn't from where he stood.

"It hasn't been redone in a while. She'll do whatever you want."

He couldn't be serious. Mylaynee said we could add our own touches, but a designer, really? I couldn't afford one. Unable to speak, I stood there struggling with his kind gesture and calculating what it would cost me.

I whipped around to see what "Monique the Ten" happened to be doing. She paraded through the space, her cell phone extended an arm's length, pushing buttons as she meandered and measured with a skilled eye.

I grabbed Linc's elbow and tugged his huge body further into the hallway, out of her view. "I can't have a designer." On tiptoes, I leaned closer to his smiling eyes, extending above my five-foot-eleven frame in bare feet. "It's fine, just the way it is."

My protest ignored, he grabbed my hand and brought it up to his lips, and proceeded to kiss each and every knuckle. *Holy smokes.* My heart swooned and goosebumps popped up all over my arms. His blue eyes sucked me in and turned me to mush. The warmth of his palm penetrated my bloodstream, heating me from the inside out.

"Don't worry about it. Tell Monique what you want, no expense spared. She'll bill my account, not you."

That remark knocked me back to reality. "I've worked here one day, I can't."

He pulled me in for a hug and then leaned back, looking me square in the eyes. "I want you to be comfortable. Sal told me what your place was like. Go in there and talk to her. Give her a chance, okay?" He brushed his thumb on my chin, hypnotizing me once again. I shook my head and attempted to get control of myself and this situation.

"Linc—"

He pinched my chin and shook it. "I insist."

Battle lost, I gave in. "*Okay.*" I tried to push him away so I could go eat crow, but he didn't budge.

"Good, see that wasn't so hard. Now, give me a smooch." He leaned in, planted a hasty peck, and when he pulled away his mouth morphed from a straight line into a cheesy smile.

"Has anyone ever told you you're weird?" Arms crossed, I lifted a brow at the persistent man.

He gazed at the ceiling and back down to me, two dimples appearing at the corners of his mouth. "Nope. Don't think anyone has. You're my first." He chucked me under the chin, his bright white teeth gleaming, and then he strolled to the elevator.

On a sigh and a grin, I went back inside and talked to Monique about my gonna-be-designer-apartment.

Chapter Eight

That evening Mylaynee and I arrived together. She said she wanted to keep me company while I prepped, but instead she became the entertainment. Miss Chatty liked to talk, but she should've been a stand-up comedian. She had us in stitches, imitating various celebrities, and cracking lame jokes that were so absurd, we couldn't help but laugh.

There were different women working with me this time. Tanya, B.B.'s roommate, looked like a hard-core biker chick. Colorful tattoos ran down one arm and peeked out from various spots along her black leather vest and mini-skirt. Her spiky blond hair, cut close to the scalp, worked well on her. Not many could pull it off without coming across as grunge.

Georgie's accent sounded French. Her streaked hair, white with two-inch pink strips all around and cut on an angle toward her chin, looked stylish on her. The most striking part—she wore a fuchsia halter dress with zippers at strategic spots, offering sneak peeks along her breasts, hips, thighs, and if she bent at a certain angle, a flash of her ass, and between her legs. Clients would salivate for sure.

Oldies rock made the prep time go by fast as we shimmied to the beat. We sang and screwed up the lyrics. Mylaynee's purposeful blurting of incorrect verses didn't help, but we had a blast.

While cleaning the last table, giant hands wrapped around my mid-section, hugging me. Linc kissed me on the ear, murmuring in it, "Did you get everything settled with Monique?"

"Yes." I discarded the rag and cleaner and turned around, so I could see him to express my gratitude. "She had a lot of great ideas."

Before I could tell him thank you, he spun me in a graceful half-circle like Fred Astaire and Ginger Rogers and back into his arms. The abrupt move had my breath rushing out and my poor heart constricting—again. His hands on my hips tightened as he pressed me against every well-defined ridge, fusing us chest to thigh. "Good. Don't forget, when you're done, come to my place." He mouthed the request across my cheek and ended in the crook of my neck.

"O-okay." Lost in some mystical fog, I uttered a nonsensical reply, "Do you want me to bring anything?"

He looked at me with a creased brow. "What do you mean?"

I lifted my shoulder and mumbled, "Uh, I-I don't know," and dropped my gaze to the floor. Why did I act like an idiot around this man?

His lips pressed to my ear again and in a sinful voice he said, "You, beautiful, bring you."

Could a person self-combust?

At my exposed shoulder, he nipped and tasted. As he did, I stretched and rubbed along him like a cat in heat.

Surely that wasn't me purring too?

He stepped back, his eyes sparkling with blatant mischief, a wicked smile pulling the right side of his mouth up. He squeezed my side, and in one swift move, turned and strolled to his office.

The view from behind couldn't be more spectacular. Without a suit jacket on, his well-fit dress pants displayed an underwear-model-butt, burning my retinas, but I couldn't look away. As he closed the door blocking the sight, my brain jolted into gear. After a shuddering sigh and a shake of my head, I got back to work.

When I approached the bar, three sets of eyes fixated on me. Mylaynee's amused, Georgie's curious, and Tanya's sneering.

"What the hell was that," Tanya snapped, crossing her tattooed arms.

My body jerked at her unexpected attack. Not knowing this chick, I decided to proceed with caution and sat on the edge of the stool next to Mylaynee. "What do you mean?"

Tanya leaned toward me. "Don't play stupid with me, girl."

Mylaynee rose from her seat and pushed Tanya's shoulder. "What the hell is your problem?"

Tanya pierced Mylaynee with a scowl. "She's the problem." She pointed to me and gripped the edge of the bar. Her knuckles whitening as if she had to hold herself back.

"Girl, you better check it. Linc finds out you're talkin' to her that way, you'll be out on your ass faster than you can breathe," Mylaynee announced before I could think of an appropriate response.

What the heck was going on? Stunned, I couldn't think of a comeback. Funny how your brain freezes in high-pressure situations.

Tanya crossed her arms, brown eyes ablaze. "I'm not the new one around here. Linc would never get rid of me. I bring in lotsa business. Not everyone does what I do."

Not sure how to respond to that, my posture remained stiff and poised for any strike on her part. Regardless of the fact she looked like a biker, I wasn't going to let someone best me. I kept my eyes on her while trying to figure out a way to defuse this situation.

Mylaynee beat me to it. She stretched her body closer to Tanya. "This *new* girl is exclusive. She isn't going anywhere. Your ass can be replaced." She snapped her fingers and in her graceful manner sat back down with total confidence.

It was so cool she had my back. I tried to send her a telepathic thanks, but she remained fixed on the target taking shots at me.

Tanya leaned so close I could smell her foul breath. "Exclusive? No way."

Mylaynee transformed to a cat that caught the canary. "Ha! Believe it," she shouted, slapping the glass top, a ricocheting thump that caused Georgie and me to flinch.

At that, I turned my head toward her, bewildered at this woman's continued defense on my behalf. Yeah, this girl could take my back any time. Awesome.

Tanya glared. "*You're* exclusive with Linc?"

I nodded and glimpsed between Tanya and Mylaynee, trying to figure out if this discussion had come to an end or if I should prepare for a bigger problem.

Tanya barked, "You got to be shittin' me." She shook her head. "Wait till B.B. finds out."

I guess Tanya wasn't ready to shut up yet. Just as I gathered my thoughts, the door to the office opened and slammed shut. Linc strolled toward us and asked, "Everything set for the night, ladies?"

In unison, we bobbed our heads.

He reached up and tugged on my hair before placing a few strands around my ear. Slow and purposeful, he inched closer and blazed a fire-scorching kiss on my lips.

Tall and imposing, he delivered a stare at Tanya that could melt the paint off walls, flicked a glance at Georgie and Mylaynee, and winked at me. "Have a good night, ladies." He exited the stunned quiet lounge, leaving a silence behind that continued long after his departure.

I'd already knocked twice, but Linc didn't answer. As I turned to leave, the door opened, and he scooped me up and tossed me over his shoulder. "Hey, put me down," I tried to yell, but the wind had been knocked out of me on impact, making my attempt more of a garbled groan.

Instead of complying with my request he chuckled all the way into the bedroom, and catapulted us onto the feather-soft bed, my stomach leaping and bouncing with our bodies. "How was your night, beautiful?"

I took several gulps of air before replying. "Busy, it flew by." My senses primed, I inspected his stretched and relaxed state. Impossible to believe, but casual wear fit him better than the custom-made suits he wore. His T-shirt had the arms cut off and a tiny slit at the top exposed the little hairs I first saw in his office. Faded black shorts displayed fabulous toned thighs that could no doubt crush a soda can in one squeeze.

Reminiscent of Hercules, his bountiful hair and sculpted frame taunted—*touch me, I dare you.*

Eager to do just that, he beat me to it by sucking on my shoulder. He slid his tongue across it, glossing over the invisible marks he outlined earlier and drawing a line along a thrumming vein on my neck. In a swift roll, he aligned me on top. My head spinning from the sensual sneak attack and his woodsy-fruity cologne, I grasped the sheets, and in the process latched on to a hunk of his free-flowing hair—both silky and soft.

"You need anything for your place?"

Obviously, his mind wasn't in the gutter like mine. I tried to ignore the hard body beneath me and downplay the effect by propping my chin in my hand, and taking my time to produce a sane response. "It's nice…and quiet. Thank you by the way for Monique." I couldn't wait to see how our combined designs turned out. Gram and I had lived on a tight budget. Our small home contained a lot of second-hand furnishings, but had been well loved. Even so, I couldn't help feel a little giddy about the thought of new and designer.

He gripped my neck and rubbed his thumb along it in tiny circles. It didn't help my concentration one bit. "Let me know if you need help with anything, okay?"

"I'm good. I told her how much I liked the couch in your office. She said she'd try to find one. If it's anything like yours I'll end up falling asleep when I'm reading."

He squinted. "You like to read?"

"*Yeah.*"

"What kind?"

Uh oh. I blushed, glancing at the wall as I mumbled, "Uh…romance novels."

His firm grip clasped my chin, redirecting it. "Don't. You can tell me anything. Don't be embarrassed or afraid."

I didn't know what to expect of someone who owned this type of business. At first, I pictured an icky Hugh Hefner, instead got luscious Linc. His drool-worthy appearance captivated me, but so did his generosity and thoughtfulness. It made me think no matter what I revealed, he wouldn't judge. He wasn't that type of man.

"I'm addicted to them. I know it sounds like I'm living in a fantasy, but the stories, even the erotic ones are great."

Did that just come out of my blabbing mouth? My face heated and must be scarlet red from the way my cheeks burned.

A wicked grin spread across his mouth. "Erotica huh? What turns you on, beautiful?"

My gaze dashed to the wall, the windows, and the floor. I dropped my face in my hands, burying them in his chest.

Ugh, he drove me crazy.

Any other woman would've performed a thousand erotic acts with this man lying beneath her. But no, what was I doing? Hiding my freaking face! *Stupid, Serena. All these years you could've had experience.* It stunk being a virgin at this moment.

He wrapped his arms around me and squeezed. "When you're ready and feel more comfortable, I want you to tell me, okay?" He kissed the top of my head.

That action seemed even more humiliating, and I sank my cheek further into his chest. He wasn't trying to embarrass me, just curious I suppose.

"Let's go to bed. You sleeping in tomorrow?"

His bulging chest felt pillow soft, making me drowsy. I could stay here all night. Right in this spot. *Did he ask me a question?*

"Roll off, let's get undressed."

My head popped up.

In one swift move, he rolled us both over, and without dropping me, propped me on my feet.

A bead of sweat trickled from my nape, down my spine, and into my panties. Yeah, like I needed more moisture there.

He took hold of both of my hands and set them on his chest.

"I want you to undress me."

Oh. My. God.

"Huh?" I squeaked.

Wake the heck up, girl. Man wants naked. Shake a leg!

He slid my hands downward at a snail's pace, resting them at the bottom of his shirt.

"Take it off," his raspy voice instructed.

Oh Lordy.

My brain engaged—happy dance commencing.

As I pulled the jersey higher, I skimmed my knuckles over each ripple on his ribs. His arms rose and gave me a full-on, front-row view of tight, ridged abs. The shirt slipped through my fingers and melted to the floor.

Damn. Double Damn. This man needed his own freaking calendar.

When you died, was it possible to go to heaven and hell?

My eyes didn't know what to examine first, but I tried to focus. The path I chose started with his broad shoulders—large enough to support you, yet soft enough to cuddle. A well-honed, wide chest with curly black hair sprinkled across it must have taken hours of weight training to sculpt into perfection. Arms pulled taut at his side, the veins curved downward at an angle and spread across his sturdy hands. The pièce de résistance and mentioned in erotica novels time and again, I called it "The trail to nirvana," and he had it dipping past the band of his shorts.

Oh yeah, girl, you needed to wake the heck up and live more. Real life was so much better.

"Now my pants, Serena," he said in a low, soft voice.

My gaze tracked the line of dark curls up to his face. The green flecks in his eyes more prominent than before, as the blue shimmered on the outer rim.

My smile wavered, and I reined it in. Lips parted, I drew in a huge gulp of air. Blood rushed to my head, making me a little lightheaded since I'd held my breath for too long.

I cleared my throat and set my hands at the top of his shorts, shocked by the bit of confidence I seemed to find. Then I dropped to my knees and looked up.

"Serena," he choked out on a gruff reply. Eyes closed, he sucked in a ragged breath. His hands clutched my shoulders and squeezed.

The view from down here and this close—spectacular. I wanted to nuzzle my nose in that spot right—there—his fine-haired belly button and then—

"Take them off."

When I glanced up, a gasp rushed out of me. His eyes— lust? No, it couldn't be. Before I had more time to think about it, his hands gripped mine and pushed. Elastic-banded shorts didn't take much force, and they pooled at his feet.

I stared at the carpet and almost laughed, because the picture of what I must look like seated, head bowed at the feet of a gorgeous man brought to mind—a concubine. My sex-starved body and brain liked taking me on this crazy journey.

"Look at me, Serena."

As if my body responded to orders given only by him, I lifted my head.

And descended to hell for sure.

Sprung free, his shaft stuck out like a divining rod, pulling every drop of saliva out of my mouth. Virgin or not, his manly goods deserved a label—IMPRESSIVE. I guess the saying had been true…big feet…big…

Trim black hair coated the base and little patches played peek-a-boo around each sac.

"Is this your first?"

His abrupt and unexpected prompt broke my trance. My attention lifted up to his watchful gaze. His hard-to-read face no doubt already knew the answer. I glanced back down, getting another eyeful before mumbling, "Yes."

"Get up, now." His tone, louder than before, had me standing in an instant.

I should've been alarmed and kept quiet, but instead spoke first. "Is something wrong?"

He shook his head and got in bed. With an arm propped behind his pillow and the comforter covering him up to his chest, he watched me like I was an intriguing and perplexing documentary.

My gaze dropped to the floor; a sinking feeling formed in my stomach. The glittery gold sparkles on my dress caught the light from the nightstand. My hands wrapped around my middle, protecting and hugging tight.

"Come to bed, Serena."

I plodded to the other side and plunked down with my back to him. The darkness outside matched my mood. *Gloomy.* Light from harbor lampposts created shadows in various spots along the boardwalk, mirroring the mystical form lying behind me, and the reflection I kept glancing at in the window.

I unzipped the dress, and it fell to my hips. Crap. I didn't wear a bra with the strapless outfit, and my string-bikini underwear was thinner and more transparent than dental floss. All my clothes were in my apartment, and I hadn't thought to bring anything up here. Nothing I could do about it now. I wasn't about to ask for something to put on and add to the humiliation. I pulled the garment underneath me and let it fall to the floor. Tomorrow, I'd plan ahead and bring something to sleep in. On my next trip to the Goodwill, I'd get a robe.

A finger skimmed my lower back. "When did you get the tramp stamp?"

Seriously? Okay, call me naive. I didn't know people called it that when I got it.

"Six months ago," I countered, like getting inked had been routine for me. Ha! He'd never know.

"What language is it? What's it say?"

I smiled and my retort rushed out before giving it much thought.

"Hmm, if I told you then I'd have to—"

He burst out laughing so hard the bed shook, registering at least six points on the Richter scale.

As I turned toward him, I made sure to keep my chest covered by my arm. "You don't think I'm serious? I have connections, you know." I giggled, because his hearty chuckles made it too hard to resist.

His arm covered his eyes as he continued to laugh, and that was all I needed to sneak under the comforter, pulling it up to my chin. I willed my mind off the deep voice that echoed in the room and the naked centerfold behind me. Yeah, good luck with that. Every movement he made seemed hardwired to my body.

His hand snaked around my waist, coming to rest between my breasts. Snuggled along my back, his bare chest and *everything* aligned at my rear. "Good night, beautiful."

I closed my eyes and hoped he couldn't feel the trembles rushing from my pinky toes to temple.

"Sweet dreams, Linc."

Chapter Nine

Bright sunlight woke me. Pillow shoved to the side, I looked for a clock. Ugh, adjusting to a new schedule stunk. My usual bedtime had been around midnight, but now it didn't come until two thirty. On days I had to be at the Millers' by seven, the less than five hours of sleep left me feeling hung over, and I didn't even drink anything. Thank goodness I'd reserved Tuesdays and Thursdays for bookkeeping, giving me a chance to sleep in. When daylight hit me though, my brain didn't agree, it decided I had enough and wanted me to get up. Great, so much for that plan.

I threw on my dress and entered the cook's dream kitchen. A note taped to the best appliance in the world caught my attention. Someone should encapsulate coffee makers in gold or platinum since they provided a treasure the majority of the population couldn't live without.

Beautiful-
Coffee's ready. Cup on counter for you. Went for run.
Linc

Holy crap, a tan mug with a green "S" on it had me grabbing the counter and my chest at the same time, a shaking hand on each. Dang it, why did he do that? If I had experience, I'd know what it meant. In two days, I'd received a brand new wardrobe, a rent-free apartment, and an interior designer who had plans to paint and install new flooring and furniture. Now this. The small gesture meant more to me than all the rest. Often, the unplanned, spontaneous deeds were the type that brought immeasurable joy and in some instances, instilled hope.

Focus, Serena—you're here for one reason. Falling for a man is not in the plan.

I needed to guard my inexperienced heart. Otherwise, I'd end up devastated when living here came to an end.

He's my boss, being nice. That's all. It's no big deal, right?

I fisted my hand and used it to knock some sense into my brain. A busy day ahead of me, I walked back to my apartment with a full mug repeating, *he's a good guy, he'd do it for anybody, it doesn't mean anything.*

Oldies rock fueled my mad typing skills as I hammered away at the accounts. Several abrupt knocks stopped my bobbing head and progress. When I opened the door, my stomach took an immediate three-and-a-half inward somersault dive. A sweaty, flushed Linc stood there with his arms spread across the narrow doorway, splaying him like an eagle soaring through the sky. He grabbed me around the waist and hauled me forward, kissing me with such vigor, I had to hold on to his hot, wet neck for dear life so I wouldn't fall as he tilted me backward.

"You aren't in my bed. What the hell?"

I stared, lips parted, still bent backward with his gorgeous, sticky body melting mine. Caught in his all-consuming, mind-bending spell, I couldn't figure out my name, the day, year, or even recite the alphabet. All my brain saw or could say—*Linc, Linc, Linc.*

My eyes did function though, and noticed two protruding nipples on his skintight T-shirt. If I took a nip right there, what would it taste like? By some miracle his question registered, and I responded after a lengthy pause. "Didn't you see what I wrote on your note?"

"No. When you weren't there, I came here." He clasped his hand in mine and pulled me into the living room, setting me on his lap. Wrapped in his arms, his body heat warmed me up even though his damp shirt seeped through mine. I couldn't care less.

"I had invoices to work on."

He nodded and stared in my eyes. I could see the wheels spinning in his brain, formulating something. "Do you like accounting?"

"Yeah, it's what I'd like to do full-time."

His hold tightened on my ribs. "Why'd you quit school?"

I wasn't expecting that, or the gigantic hole bursting wide open in my heart when he asked it. Avoidance became my best option, and the turquoise butterflies flitting across the computer screensaver looked fascinating enough, better than his expectant stare. When I didn't answer, he grasped my chin and redirected it toward him. "I told you, don't be embarrassed or afraid to tell me anything."

Yeah, easier said than done. Uncomfortable where the conversation might lead, I got up and approached the folders stacked twenty high. "I'd rather not talk about it." I picked up a pencil, about to scribble a note in a client's file, when he removed it from my grasp, tossing it down. It kept rolling and plopped on the floor, right where my eyes remained.

He grabbed my hand and squeezed it, his voice gentler and softer when he spoke again. "What happened, Serena?" His eyes, a sky blue today, showed very little green. Weird how they seemed to change whenever we talked. Maybe they were like mood rings.

My attention shifted to our joined hands, his bigger and darker than mine, they didn't look odd together. In fact, they fit better than puzzle pieces, different in every way, but connecting perfectly.

If the situation with Monique had taught me anything, he wouldn't give up anytime soon. "My gram had cancer." I took a deep breath and exhaled before continuing. "Things didn't go well. I wanted to take care of her, so I didn't go back to school."

He placed the sweetest kiss on my temple, whispering in the same spot, "I'm so sorry." His warm, strong arms wrapped around my back, making me feel safe, protected. The harbor view and heat still radiating from his body eased my nerves somewhat. My excessive blinking resisted the tears that wanted to fall. No doubt it would turn this into an embarrassing situation rather than a supportive one. When would the pain stop?

"Why do you have three jobs?"

Damn, this interrogation just ventured into "plead the fifth" territory. For a year I'd kept the real reason a secret, and if I could, no one would *ever* know. Gram would roll over in her grave if she knew why I lost the house she left me in her will. Someday I'd have to deal with it. I needed money though, tons of it, to unravel the huge mess. To keep him from asking any more prying questions, I formulated a half-true version that would reveal a teensy bit and satisfy his curiosity.

"My gram didn't have insurance. We used credit cards, took out loans for medical and college expenses." I traced an absent-minded pattern on the seam of his jersey while explaining. "Payments got to be too much. I kept up with the accounting and worked for the Millers, but spent most of my time taking care of her."

Quiet for a while, his breathing sounded louder than the honking boat outside. "You could start over. File for bankruptcy."

I glared at him and stated matter-of-factly, "No, I'm not doing that." Tired of the conversation, I went out to the balcony. I needed some fresh air.

Linc came up next to me and nodded toward a boat. "You been sailing?"

His abrupt change in subject took me by surprise. "No, I plan to though. It's on my wish list."

He turned toward me with a repressed smirk. "You're a planner, huh?"

His question and the teasing way he said it made me chuckle, lightening the tension. "Yeah, you got a problem with that?"

A smile stretched across his face as he wrapped his arms around my stomach and placed his chin on my head. Rays of sunshine rolled along the gentle current, mesmerizing me with the lolling motion. Birds' sweet tweets echoed in rhythm to the beating waves, adding to the calming scene. Warm temperatures and his heated chest turned me to mush, like chocolate left in the sun too long. A slight breeze caressed my face and brought with it a fresh-cut grass smell, reminding me spring would be here soon. Five weeks from now, April first, I'd be twenty-two. If the date didn't speak volumes about my life, I didn't know what did.

He cleared his throat, his Adam's apple rubbing against the back of my head. "Since you're not catering anymore, the money you make bartending, you could give up the nanny job." He ducked his head, pressing his lips against my ear. "Let me help you, Serena. I have business contacts everywhere. One call and they'll send accounts your way. Would you like that?"

I closed my eyes and listened to his even breaths. His strong arms, steady and sure, made everything seem so simple. But Gram's *you don't get something for nothing* mentality and die-hard work ethic had instilled a self-determination I couldn't ignore. It might take time, but my problems would get resolved, and I had to do it without people stepping in and rescuing me. In some way, maybe she'd see the granddaughter she raised as her own had learned a lot. Her fighting spirit a good one to emulate. "Never give up. Tackle one problem at a time, big or small. Challenges cultivate the soul, reaping a prosperous harvest." Her words of wisdom came at the most unusual times, and encouraged and invigorated me.

A first-generation immigrant, she had many traditions and insights from her Welsh upbringing. She taught me the language and established customs I still followed. The dragon tattoo and quote on my back, a tribute and evidence of her influence. Her positive attitude became my anchor. She demonstrated what I strive to be: caring, compassionate, and independent.

Perhaps the charming man waiting for an answer entered my life to teach me a few things too. Unlike what I'd envisioned, his generosity and thoughtfulness blindsided me. Mylaynee had been right. He would take care of me, but I couldn't let him.

"The Millers depend on me. They have three young kids, and it's not easy to find someone else. Besides, I've been working for them a long time. When Gram passed, Mrs. Miller added more days to my schedule so I could make extra money. I won't ditch them."

"Let me make some calls then."

God, I didn't know why it felt so right to be with him, but it did. I set my hand on his cheek, brushing the stubble. His sincerity and heartfelt gaze formed a lump in my throat. "I appreciate the offer, but I'll handle it."

His cell phone rang, and he silenced it.

"It's okay. I have to get back to work. Take your call." I gave him a peck on each cheek and went inside, sitting at the computer. I turned to grab the next folder, and Linc snuck in, planting another dizzying, lingering kiss on me. Phone extended away from his ear, the sing-song voice was unmistakable—B.B. She continued to talk, but I couldn't make out the gibberish, because my Linc-addicted brain wiped her out.

I had to give him credit. He was thorough and gave more than he got. He rolled his tongue back and forth on the roof of my mouth and drifted it side to side, playing "tag, you're it," leading me on a wild goose chase. Every kiss upped the stakes and made me crave him no matter the cost. Maybe he should sell his carnal techniques on the black market. He'd never have to work another day in his life.

An annoying beep tugged me from the blissful moment. Instead of pulling way, Linc nibbled along my swollen bottom lip, nipped my chin, and pecked the ridge of my jaw on his way to my earlobe, where he flicked and sucked. Our bodies touched nowhere else except where his firm grasp molded my hands to the armrests. He took a step back, the dead call buzzing in the room stung and left a bitter taste in my mouth as he tucked the phone in his pocket all casual-like and smooth. That act produced a tsunami of clarity and perspective, slapping me out of my euphoria. My position in an awkward forming triangle, caught in-between Linc and B.B., caused me to squirm in my seat.

"Bring some clothes to my place." As I watched him mosey out, the dull thud of the closing door replicated the sound that repeated in the room when I dropped my head on the computer desk. Another example of why I was born on April first. My middle name should've been fool instead of

Angelique. One stupid move after another amplified the pit in my stomach. Dang it, I didn't need any more problems. Disgusted with myself, I snatched a file off the stack and logged the entries in a spreadsheet.

Concentrate on work, nothing else.

Hours later, I threw on a track suit and took off for a jog, returning to my old stomping grounds. At the end of the sidewalk, I stared at the overgrown yard and vacant house. It looked different without lights on, without two females sitting on the front porch, without the wood blinds open...

Without Gram.

Without me.

Without...even the sun.

It had come out earlier but now remained hidden, concealed by a misty fog that rolled in about an hour ago, shielding my homestead and shrouding it in a haze.

Right there. My reminder. My purpose. My intent.

Fired up, I ran full blast, determined nothing and *no one* would get in my way.

Chapter Ten

Sunday and my first day off began with Mylaynee pounding on my door at the crack of dawn, rocking on the balls of her feet. "So what are we doing today?"

"Uh, I'm not sure. I need another cup of coffee before I can think straight." I walked to the kitchen for a refill. "Want some?"

"No, I don't drink that stuff."

I pretended shock at her claim. "I'll have *three* then, one just for you." She giggled all the way to the balcony. We plopped down in the plastic chairs and propped our feet on the rail as we watched the whitecaps. Hypnotized by the ripples, I wracked my brain for something we could do. In under a week I'd made at least one friend, and maybe over time I'd have a few more. Mylaynee situated herself into my life, making the transition smoother and happier than I could've predicted. An idea forming, I asked, "Do you like animals?" ·

Her scrunched brows and hesitant answer didn't show much confidence. "Yes."

I took a sip from the steamy mug before responding, building the suspense. "Have you gone horseback riding?

Croton Point Park offers trail rides on the weekends, and it's not too expensive."

She sat up taller, her feet dropping from the railing. "No I haven't, but I'd like to try. Have you gone?"

"Gram and I used to sometimes."

She grabbed my hand and gave it a gentle squeeze. "We could do something else."

I shook my head. "No, I need this, but thank you." My smile widened to reassure her.

She leapt across, wrapping her arms around my shoulders and squeezing tight. "Okay, then. What do I wear?" she said on a rush, glancing down at her bright white, steam-pressed linen outfit.

I laughed because I hadn't seen her in jeans or anything that could be considered casual. My smile got larger as I envisioned her wearing my thrift store garb. "Let's go look in your closet and see what we can find."

After rooting through her massive collection, we found out that cowgirl duds most definitely did not come in designer labels.

Mylaynee insisted on buying a cowboy hat and boots on our way there. The little kids on the trail ride got a kick out of her as she sang out-of-tune country songs the entire time. It didn't take long for the others to join in too. She had me in stitches so much that tears flowed non-stop. Joyful ones and exactly what I needed.

Not a second off the horse, she announced another activity, taking me to a different type of park not far from Croton Point. Sweat dripped from my hairline as I tilted my head back and locked sights on the towering monster she made a beeline for as soon as we got there. I regretted in that instant, agreeing to her idea. My stomach twisted in knots as I peered at my worst fear—the Ferris wheel.

"I don't think I can ride that. The sign says it goes six hundred thirty feet in the air and carries up to fourteen hundred people. What's with those capsule things? Where's the seats? I'm dizzy and we haven't even gotten on it yet," I whined with scaredy-cat perfection.

She looped her arm through mine and tugged me forward. My hand cupped over my brow forming an imitation sun shield, I examined every inch. Crap, *much* worse than I thought.

"It's brand new. First season. Want me to hold your hand?" she teased.

"Oh, so we're crash dummies now? I know you love amusement parks, I'm right there with ya, but look how high it goes, for cripes sake!" My shouting got louder the closer we got, and I pointed upward as if she couldn't see it.

"Geesh, girl, live a little." She hip checked me, making me stumble. Her determined grasp on my arm kept me from falling; all the while she giggled and chanted, "You can do it, you can do anything." Her smart-alecky remark and grin didn't help one bit. My mini panic attack grew to new heights, matching the towering monstrosity. She didn't give my rant another thought and tugged me to the end of the line.

Faster than I'd hoped, the ticket taker motioned for us to enter the glass cylinder. As my feet shuffled inside, I sucked in just as many breaths of artificial air as steps taken. When we came to a stop, I leaned my gonna-die weight against Mylaynee, hoping she'd hold me up if I passed out. After about fifty or so people were locked in, the ride moved upward at a snail's pace. New York City and the Manhattan skyline spread across a never-ending canvas. Mylaynee's hand flashed in front of me, pointing at the bay. "I love Staten Island. You been here before?"

"Yeah, a few times, but I don't get on stuff like this, and wouldn't if you didn't force me." I gave her the evil eye, and she laughed at my half-baked attempt to look upset.

"Relax, girl. I'll make you a deal. You can pay me back some day. Besides, I wanted to share it with you."

Yeah, I did need to enjoy it, since there was no way in hell I'd get on it again. She threw an arm over my shoulder and pulled me tighter to her side, like best buds. We shared the view with our heads propped against one another. The Verrazano–Narrows Bridge, Lady Liberty, Ellis Island, and the Staten Island 9/11 memorial gave us glimpses of the past and present. From this vantage point, the closer the wheel brought us the more chills I got on my arms. I glanced at Mylaynee, her wet cheeks said the awful memories of that day affected her too. "My heart hurts every time I see those wings. That's what they look like to me anyway," she whispered and I nodded in agreement.

"Life's so short," I muttered, and on a silent breath said a prayer for all the people who lost their lives, including one for those who loved them.

The afternoon flew by as we ate elephant ears, chased each other through the fun house and rode everything in the park, almost. On my dare, Mylaynee tried to sweet-talk a conductor into letting her get on the kiddie go-carts. He patted her on the shoulder and shooed her away. We giggled, recited silly knock-knock jokes, and acted like schoolgirls. I never realized what I'd missed before. Gram fulfilled a big part and her friends were great, but today proved I needed to reach out and form friendships with other people around my age.

At Mylanee's apartment, we each claimed a couch and vegetated after a fun-filled and exhausting afternoon. Classic movies chosen from her vast collection, I relaxed and ate junk food, willing my eyes to stay open through the scenes. Out of the blue, something plunked me in the head. I glanced down; a piece of popcorn was stuck in between my boobs. "Ha ha, real funny. Do I need to take your treat away, little girl?"

Her hysterical giggle followed me across the room. I plopped down next to her and she nudged her shoulder into mine. "We had fun, huh?"

I kept my eyes glued on the large screen TV and replied with my best monotone voice. "Nah, I could've had better."

A handful of popcorn hit me in the face. Miss Gonna-Get-Her-Ass-Kicked dashed away, hiding behind the other couch.

Stunned by her ridiculousness, it took me a second to get with the program. "Food fight!" I yelled and snatched fistfuls of strawberries and grapes, whipping them at her. Loud banshee cries erupted as we darted from one piece of furniture to the next, ducking, throwing, and diving again. I tried to keep her from getting to the center table with all the reinforcements, but quick-witted Mylaynee had other ideas. She darted into the kitchen and came out wielding a new weapon.

My hands flew up in the air in total surrender. "Mother May I, Simon Says, and any other safe words." I ducked into a closet and peeked through the crack, suppressing the laugh I wanted to let out. "If I had a white towel I'd hold it out. Come on, Mylaynee, you started it. I'm done, no more, honest. I'm not taking another shower tonight."

When I looked again, she smiled real wide, tilted the canister upside down, and squirted a mouthful of whipped cream inside, swirling it upward in a curly-cue sundae topping design. "You're nuts, you know that?" I sat in my original seat, far away from the loony-bin side. Her manic, full-mouth giggles made me laugh too. I watched her, amazed she didn't choke on the massive amounts she'd jammed in there.

After she swallowed several times and licked her lips, she set her hands on her hips and demanded, "You're gonna help clean up, right?"

"You started it, you should have to do it. But since I'm such a *nice* person, I'll lend a hand," I said in a sickening sweet way.

"We better get started then. I'm sure Linc's wondering where you are."

My grin vanished, turning into a jaw-crunching scowl.

"What's wrong?" She sat beside me, tucking her legs underneath and pulling my hand into her lap in a comforting gesture. "Spill it. That's what girlfriends are for."

"Okay." I glanced at the TV, contemplating what I wanted to say. "When I woke up, he was gone. That's not unusual since he works out in the morning. He left a note saying he wouldn't see me until tomorrow night."

"Hmm, he's not the chatty type. So I don't know what to tell ya."

I remained quiet, curious about where he could've gone and not sure what else to say. We'd known each other for six days, but it felt longer. Sleeping alone tonight would feel strange. His naked body molded to my back and hand between my breasts seemed like the most natural thing in the world, as if a ritual had taken root and been growing for a hundred years. The first couple nights, it unsettled me, but by the third, he became my very own made-just-for-me-heated-blanket.

The attraction, the desire, the need to be with him got harder to ignore. Even with my firm plan in place, his daily presence messed with my head and my body. So far my job involved bartending and sleeping in his bed every night. No sex. What did that mean?

Mylaynee's sweeping under my feet brought me out of my daydream. I didn't even realize she'd gotten up. "So you gonna sit there all night and pout like some lovesick teenager?" She pointed to the messiest spot, where I'd thrown the fruit. "You have to clean that side."

"You know…" I bounced up and took the broom from her hands. "You sound like a pain-in-the-butt big sister."

She pecked me on the cheek and then pinched it. "Thanks, lil' sis, love ya." Her mega-watt smile and sweet declaration lightened my heart.

I pulled her into a bear hug, and knew right then and there I had a friend for life.

Chapter Eleven

An envelope under the door revealed my first paycheck—woo-hoo! I made it one week. Good to his word, the check had one thousand dollars written across it. With the eight hundred I'd made in tips, my net turned out triple what I would have earned catering in the same amount of time.

Later, I'd do some calculating and figure out which bills to tackle first. I'd have to hire an attorney or private investigator in the future and deal with my biggest headache. Just thinking about it made my blood boil. The longer I let the issue go unanswered the worse it got. Avoiding it for much longer wasn't wise, but dealing with it now wasn't possible either. I'd buried the past a long time ago, and if I opened the wound now, it would bleed me dry. Yeah, like it hadn't already.

I glanced down at the check and the LBJ, Inc. stamped in the corner. How did it work, I wondered? He'd have to conceal this place from the IRS. A dummy corporation? I chuckled. What the heck did I know? Mylaynee mentioned he'd been doing this about eight years. What would make him do it? It wasn't like you woke up one day and said, "Hey,

Mom and Dad, I want to go into business. Oh, by the way, I'm gonna open a sex club."

Aargh, I had tons of things to accomplish today. On the agenda, jog to the bank, deposit the check, and get some bills paid.

Plan formulated.

And executed.

I stepped off the elevator and found B.B. pounding on my door.

"Is something wrong?"

She whipped toward me and crossed her arms. "You got some nerve, bitch," she ground out between lips colored a disgusting Pepto-Bismol pink.

Not this again. First Tanya, now her. Well, I had enough of this bull. "Is there a problem?" I asked in a sugar-sweet voice.

She spat out through clenched teeth, "He. Is. Not. Your. Man."

Huh? Honestly, if I didn't want to make things worse I would've laughed in her pissed- off face. My rule, avoid confrontation. I took a few steps back, tightening my muscles for any impending attack. "If you have a problem with that you need to take it up with Linc, not me. I'm here to do my job." Irritated by this whole ordeal, I turned my back on her and tried to fit the key in the door. Not finished with me, she grabbed my shoulder and shoved me, knocking it out of my hand and blocking my entry. I growled, "Don't touch me again," and bent down to pick up the key. As soon as I clasped it in my palm, she stomped her wedged sandal on my curled hand, crunching it into the carpet.

When I glanced up, she clenched the door frame and exerted more pressure, cementing my hand to the floor. "I'm the only *exclusive* he's got or needs. I'm his woman—before…" Crunch. "during…" Grinding harder. "and after."

Abrupt and to the point I warned, "I'll tell you what, take your foot off my hand right now, and I'll let you walk away…*without a bloody face.*"

She tilted her head back and burst into a throaty cackle, grinding her shoe along my knuckles and scraping the protruding bones.

Every muscle in my upper body tightened, and on a full-force upswing, my fist blindsided her snickering mouth, landing a roundhouse punch to her nose.

Multiple reactions resulted almost simultaneously—she screamed bloody murder, cupped her nose, removed her shoe from my aching hand, and began to creep backward as blood gushed down her shocked face.

As I straightened from my bent position, doors opened at her screeching. I flexed my sore knuckles, willing the blood flow to return. B.B. entered her apartment, leaving a disgusting bloody trail along the tan carpet.

Mylaynee rushed down the hallway that still echoed with faint wails and positioned herself next to me, my supportive friend. The other women took in the after effects and closed their doors. Evidently they weren't concerned with the altercation or didn't want to get involved.

"What the hell happened?" She looked between my face and B.B.'s door, shaking her head at the red stream.

"You wanna come inside? I'd rather not discuss it out here." Not waiting for her reply, I turned the key, leading her to the living room. She sat next to me on the sofa as I plopped my feet on an ottoman and reclined my head on the back of the couch. I looked at her and shrugged with nonchalance. "She pissed me off."

"Uh, you think? What's that about?" she inquired, smirking like an eager child in a candy store loaded with an armful and anticipating a night filled with juicy treasures.

"She has a problem with me and Linc. I told her to take it up with him. She didn't like my answer and crushed my hand with her foot. I warned her, she didn't listen, so I clocked her."

She twisted toward me and confided, "She's got a thing for him, been wantin' him a long time."

"Figures."

"She hasn't been here long, but we never hit it off. I don't like her and the other girls don't either. She's worse since she got buddy-buddy with Tanya. Those two are trouble." She shook her head and advised, "I'd steer clear if I was you."

If she thought so, then I would, but I hadn't done anything to invite their anger. "I'm not here to create problems, but I'm not gonna let anyone bulldoze me either. I'm here to work, that's it."

"Girl, your job is fucking hot." She fanned her face. "He keeps his distance, and that just makes him more irresistible. Fair warning, it's not just B.B. gunnin' for him."

"Hmm...has he been with any of them?" Uncertain whether I wanted to know or not, but unable to help myself, I watched her face for the slightest revelation.

She leaned closer, setting a hand on my knee and confided, "I know they've tried. I'm not gonna lie. They talk about clients and experiences. As long as I've been here though, I've never seen him touch any of them that way. Except *you*," she emphasized, pinching my chin and shaking it.

I stared at a nonexistent spot on the wall, finding her claim hard to believe. What man wouldn't indulge? No way a sexually charged male like Linc could resist. Although, he sure did with me. Shoot, maybe he wasn't attracted to an average woman...or virgins.

Mylaynee squeezed my knee, pulling me out of my disconcerting thoughts. "Don't worry about it, Serena. Whatever happened before you is in the past. When you two are in the same room he can't keep his eyes and hands off you. I can tell you feel something for him. Just take it slow, see what happens, okay?"

My eyes closed, and I confessed, "He's getting to me. I'm inexperienced and maybe that's all it is—a crush—lust, but it scares me. I've never been in a relationship before, and I don't even know what this is." I sat up and clasped my hands together, making them hurt worse. As I rubbed them I tried to explain my convoluted feelings. "It's different here. I mean, he's paying me...and B.B., she says they're together." I watched Mylaynee, hoping for the best but planning for the worst.

She folded her legs up, tucking them behind her on the couch. "First, B.B. is full of shit." A gush of air left my lungs. "Second, he's paying you, yeah, but think about it this way. You've been bartending, right?" Not waiting for a reply she continued. "So he's payin' you to serve drinks. Claiming you as exclusive, to me it's like he wants you to be his girlfriend." Her words dug in, but I still didn't speak. "Don't think about what he's payin' you for. That isn't what you should focus on."

I processed what she said and tried to put it in some perspective. But with the drama in the hall and a never-ending hurricane named Linc, my brain twisted and whirled.

Caught in the middle of a storm, my response had been nothing...for now.

The office door opened, and Tanya exited, followed by a much shorter, stout bald man and Linc. As they wove through the lounge, Linc's eyes remained steady on mine. He tipped his chin up, acknowledging me, and followed them out.

Damn, that couldn't be good. I bet B.B. spouted a bunch of bull about her condition. What would Linc say? Would he be upset? *Oh God*, would he fire me?

Crap, I didn't have time to think about it. I still had plenty to do and the doors would be open in a few minutes. My attention redirected, I got back to work.

Paulette and Sage worked alongside me. They seemed nice, so I invited them to stop by and hang out sometime. I planned to be here a while, so I'd rather make friends, not enemies. Hmph, after the B.B. fiasco, I'd be lucky to still have a job.

Couples gathered on the dance floor and the temperature in the room got hotter in more ways than one. Dirty dancing I'd never seen before even in movies kept pulling my attention away from the three rows thick of non-stop orders. Clients acted like they'd been in the desert and were suffering from dehydration. Everyone drank a lot, including the women. No wonder—gyrating and twerking took a lot of muscle energy. Lord forbid they cramp up and lose out on an impending orgasm. Geez, my virgin eyes couldn't take much more. Maybe I should take notes.

A blond guy with an expression that said he knew he had it goin' on motioned me over. The same one I'd seen Mylaynee with and had yet to ask her about. I leaned over the bar and asked, "Can I get you anything?"

"Jack neat." His phone sex operator voice buzzed in my ear, sending a shiver down my back. Men—damn they were potent.

I fixed his drink and placed it in front of him. Before I could remove my hand, he clasped his on top. Our fingers joined, he lifted the glass, ran his tongue along his bottom lip then swallowed the entire contents. His blue eyes never left mine. *Whoa!*

He set the empty on the bar, but didn't release my hand. Instead, he pushed his mouth to my ear and asked, "What's your name, beautiful?"

Blankness—what did he say? Pupils in pinpoints, the color so light blue, it felt like I took a swim in the Caribbean.

"Name."

My eyes closed and registered what he said. I breathed a faint response he couldn't have heard over the thrumming music. "Serena."

His body shook, and it sunk in that he found my catatonic state hilarious. "Jax." I had no issue hearing him, because his lips spelled each letter and sound against my ear. I couldn't miss it or the vibrations resounding in my eardrum.

Damn. I pulled away and slipped my hand out of his. About to respond, I looked up from those piercing eyes to Linc's peering over top of him. He pitched his head to the right, pointed to his office, and moved on, expecting me to follow him.

The hunk left behind, I informed Sage of my break. The closer I got to his door, the more my nerves hopped. As much as I wanted to delay this, I knocked once and entered. He looked regal behind his desk; hands clenched on top, face expressionless, not revealing a clue. I sat and waited for him to speak.

"I just got back from B.B.'s."

I didn't talk, just listened, expecting him to elaborate and deliver my punishment. Gram always taught me to respect authority. Since I was an employee, even though I kinda slept with him, he got my full attention—as the boss.

"She told me an interesting story."

I didn't move, just remained mindful. Again, no reply.

He leaned back and cut to the chase. "She said you attacked her."

Taken aback, I shifted around in my seat and calculated a response. "That's interesting." I reinforced my shoulder against the padded armchair, trying to gauge his position and how he might respond to employees not getting along.

"Come over here, Serena," he commanded, but in a very soft voice, pointing down to the empty space beside his desk.

I shuffled forward, similar to my death-defying Ferris wheel movements. When I got closer, he grabbed my twisting hands and pulled me into his lap, cradling me in his arms. "What happened?"

"Linc…I hope you'll understand, but I'd like to keep it between me and B.B." I scanned his face, but he masked it so well I had no idea the outcome. I'd never been in trouble at work before, so this was new to me.

He leaned back, and the chair tilted with our combined weight, knocking me off balance and bumping my shoulder into his chin. I began to get up but his hold on me tightened, locking me in place. "Let me know if I need to intervene." His response calm and sure, punctuated with a peck to my temple.

Heart lightened some, my wringing hands relaxed in my lap. Stunned by his understanding nature and the fact he didn't fire me for assaulting another employee, I remained speechless, nodding my reply.

"There's something else we need to talk about." His ominous tone and hundred eighty- degree change made the air stuffy, and his tightened arms strangled my waist, forcing the breath from my lungs. On high alert, my spine stiffened and my fingers and toes cramped from clenching over and over. No idea where this might be headed, I let him speak first, again.

"Stay away from Jax."

My mind flitted to the bar and what he must have seen. Crap. I didn't know what to say, so I nodded again.

He must have accepted it, because he reverted to our first topic. "B.B. can't work tonight, and I have a client interested in Sage. Paulette's there. You two okay or do you need help?"

Grateful for the reprieve and ready to get back to work, I quick-stepped it toward the exit. "We're good. You want me to get Sage?"

"No, beautiful, I'll be out in a minute and introduce her."

On that note, I scooted out, unsettled by the events and the entire exchange. An ache growing in my head warned of an impending migraine.

Get your act together, Serena. Don't screw this up.

"You ready to go?" Paulette asked after drying the last glass. "You look like you're gonna fall over."

"I'm so ready for bed. These hours are killing me." I kicked off my heels and looped the straps around my fingers. "I have to get Linc. Go ahead without me. I'll turn the lights off."

"You sure? I could wait."

"Nah, go. He wants me to walk back with him."

She laughed and tossed the towel on the counter. "Yeah, *he* wants you to." She winked and waved on her way out. "See ya.

Don't do anything I wouldn't do," she yelled loud enough to be heard in the next town.

I nudged the door open and came to an abrupt stop. B.B. had both hands jammed in Linc's long hair, sucking his face off. His back to me, neither noticed I'd entered. My heart lodged in my throat. Unable to stomach another second, I dashed back to my apartment.

After a lot of tossing and turning, exhaustion somersaulted me into an intense dream about a knight in shining armor. Distant pounding pulled me out of it. Groggy, I rolled over and covered my head with a pillow, but the hammering didn't stop. What the heck? I peeked at the clock—four in the morning. *Ugh, go away.* A bang and thump like someone kicked my door down got me out of bed.

Drowsy, I stutter-stepped down the hall and squinted through the peephole. I flipped the lock, and before I could turn the knob, Linc rushed in, scooting me back to my warm mattress. Too tired to argue or talk, I crawled in and collapsed.

In the distance, I heard him discarding clothes. He slid in behind me and spooned my back, whispering, "Go back to sleep, Serena." He nuzzled my neck devotedly, and I did as he said.

Chapter Twelve

My alarm blared with an insistent beep. Warm cozy arms snuggled around me, pulling me backward while I hit the off button. In the same motion something else got turned on. Or should I say, *someone.* Linc draped his leg over top of mine, and trailed butterfly kisses across my shoulder, along my neck, and made an emergency landing on my lips. Greeting—*good morning,* Linc style.

I mumbled against his insistent mouth, "Shower. Millers." He froze and dropped his face in the pillow. "Get up." His steady breathing and closed eyes could've been mistaken for sleeping, but I knew better. Hmph, big faker.

Draped over me like a human blanket, I inched an arm loose and pinched his side. "Linc—" I couldn't contain the snort that escaped. "I mean it. I have to go. *Move.* You're crushing me."

No response.

I pushed on his ribs, demanding, "I…" shove, "can't…" nudging my chin into his shoulder, "get…" smacking his butt, "up…" bucking beneath the behemoth I yelled, "with *you* on me." Uncontrollable giggles took over as he pressed two hundred-plus pounds into me, smashing me flat against the mattress and knocking any remaining oxygen out my body. "You're making me late. Move, I can't breathe." My plea sounded like gurgling water since I tried to suck in air while laughing and talking at the same time.

He cracked up too. His hot and husky baritone tickled my ear and other primed intimate spots, every one of my muscles thrumming from waves of aftershocks as his body rocked against mine. Dang it. During his next disappearing act, my vibrator would be getting a lot of attention.

He picked up his head; long, black hair nestled each side of my face—*irresistible*. Damn him. He smelled like heaven in the morning, and I no doubt had goat breath.

Oh God, he's going to make me fall in love with him.

I called myself every foul name in the book. Get a clue, girl, B.B. had him. Face the facts.

He rolled to the other side, crossing an arm over his brow.

I jumped up and shuffled toward the bathroom. Unable to resist, I glanced back and examined the charming man who had no idea the power he had to destroy my naive heart.

He peeked out from under his arm. "I'll make coffee and bring it to you."

Once I'd escaped to the bathroom, I sank to the floor and dropped my head into my shaking hands. A screeching, frustrated scream echoed in the enclosed space, and right now, I didn't care one bit if he heard me.

Yep, one more complication to add to the list.

High gas prices and the fact I needed to save money compelled me to jog most places. Linc's morning antics put me behind schedule, and I had no choice but to drive. After I saw my car, I called Mrs. Miller and told her I'd be late.

Mylaynee opened her door with a fruit drink in hand, her version of morning java. "Hey, girl, I thought you'd be gone by now."

"Yeah, me too. I have a flat. Can you drive me?"

"Sure, let me get my keys. I have some packages to drop off at the post office anyway." She handed me a box, picked up another one, and snatched her purse. "Let's go."

When we got in the garage she pointed at my tire. "You should call Linc. He'll fix it and come get you later."

"I'm not botherin' him. Besides, I'll run back, it's no big deal."

"Okay, but don't say I didn't warn you. He'll want to help, that's how he is. And since it's you, he'll be pissed you didn't tell him."

I shrugged and ignored her. It wasn't a big deal. I could handle simple car repairs. He had other stuff to worry about, and I doubt he'd get bent out of shape over something so trivial.

After we got in her cool sports car, she revved the engine and drove me to work, breaking every speed limit and racing record known to mankind.

I got several calls on my way home, resulting in four new accounts. I asked how they found out about me, and even though their explanations seemed logical, they were unusual. Maybe Lady Luck took pity, throwing me a bone. Or it might be a trend, and just the help I needed to hire an attorney sooner rather than later.

I jogged into the garage, popped the trunk and removed the jack and spare. As I loosened the lug nuts with a socket wrench, a shuffle behind me brought the quick repair job to a stop. The bald man from last night stood a few feet behind me.

"You're Serena, right?" His huge smile looked overly pleased.

On a nod, I rose. "Yes, I'm sorry, I don't know your name. We haven't been introduced."

His solid grip shook my slightly dirty hand. "Sal, I'm in charge of security."

Since he'd accompanied Linc and Tanya, he must know what I'd done. Nothing like making a bad first impression. He probably thought I was a bully and put me on his radar as a person to watch. Great, he must've come down here for that.

"I see." My response came out clipped and cold. Alright, I shouldn't be such a witch. He hadn't said anything about it. No reason for him to have a worse opinion of me. "It's good to meet you then. I'm sorry, but I need to get back to this." I pointed to the still-flat tire. Geez, that sounded bitchy too.

He scratched his bald head. "Why are you doing that?"

"Uh…because it needs fixed."

His wide grin exposed nicotine-stained teeth. "The security guys can do that. Hell, Linc would do it." His beefy frame stood proud and conveyed a message I'd interpreted as *changing a flat tire is man's work.*

"I appreciate the offer, but I can change it myself."

He crossed his arms, shaking his head side to side. His hearty chuckles bounced off the cement walls.

"What's so funny?" I tapped my foot at his chauvinistic attitude.

He glanced up. "Nothing, doll." He stroked his fingers along a scraggly chin and announced, "I can see why the boss likes you so much."

Ridiculous. I turned my back on him and picked up the wrench, twisting it up and down real fast.

Still laughing as if it were comedy hour, he relayed, "I'll let you get back to it then. See ya around, Serena."

After he left, I mumbled, "Guys can do that," my snarky parroting made me feel a whole lot better. Task completed in under five minutes, I clapped my hands once at a job well done.

Ha! Stuff it you know where, baldy.

A much-needed shower on my mind, I threw open the door and found beach-Barbie B.B. lounging on my sofa and glaring over her purple honker. I gave myself a mental pat on the back. In a bad mood from the Sal show, I had no patience left.

"What the hell are you doin' here?" My feet locked in the entryway, I stood my ground.

She dangled a crystal heart key ring. "I used to live here before moving in with Tanya." She smirked, spinning it around her finger. "I still have a key."

"And you didn't think to return it to Linc or me when I moved in." I pointed to her and back to the hallway. "Get out."

She scooted her back along the couch and tossed her feet on the ottoman. "I'm not going anywhere until we talk," she declared, crossing her arms.

What a freaking witch. Both strong-willed women, it didn't mix well under normal circumstances, and this wasn't a normal situation. "I have nothing to say to you."

She dropped her flip-flop covered feet with a thump and stood. "I have *plenty* to tell you." Her head emphasized each word. "I'll make this easy, so you can understand." She enunciated each syllable real slow like I had zero I.Q.

Determined not to let her antagonize me, I stayed steady and in place.

Her hands whipped out to her sides, she waved them top to bottom along her body like the models on the Price is Right. "*This* is not…" She pointed a painted index finger at me. "*That,*" she spat as if tasting a vial of shit. "*You* will *never* satisfy him. I can, will, and do. I know he comes to you, but he's with me, in my bed, having *sex-with-me.* Not—" Her mouth transformed into a Cheshire Cat expression as she purred, "a *virgin.*" She strutted toward me. "*You* don't cut it here."

Shit, hold it together. My chin dropped to my chest along with my hair, shielding my face. I stared at the floor and hoped she didn't see the red-hot heat creeping up my neck. The truth rocked me to the core. It ripped open and exposed a gaping wound inside me that wouldn't be easy to repair. Remember why you're here. Don't let her ruin it. My grip tightened on the doorknob, willing her to get the hell out. My brain worked in spits and spatters, and by some miracle I pitched an out-of-my-ass tactful response: "I need to get to work."

She planted herself half a foot away and dug the dagger even deeper. "All mine. Pay attention, you already missed the boat. Exclusive—not. Temporary—yes." She strutted across the hall, then turned and faced me. "I'm the queen. His partner in bed and in business. Soon, I'll be managing the girls, and you'll have to answer to *me*."

Bite. Your. Tongue. I held my hand out to her challenging face and waited for my key. She looked down at it and then back up. With a quirk to her brow, she stepped up to me and dropped it in my hand. I clenched it closed, the jagged ridges biting into my palm.

She leaned up to my ear, and for a minute I thought she was going to bite me, so I lunged back. She mocked, "Who do you think he's with on Sundays when he's gone all day, all night?"

Face blank, a seething fire erupted in my belly from my repressed anger. I motioned with my key-filled fist to her door. "*Don't* come back."

Jaw clenched, she stared at me and then stomped across the hall. The slamming door rocked her bitter stink against me.

I flipped her off and rushed inside. Her stench and our exchange scrubbed off in the shower, but the awful reality of my boss with that wench didn't wash. It lingered and festered.

Chapter Thirteen

Fallon didn't mind my late arrival. I told her about my flat tire and the whole Sal debacle but didn't mention anything about B.B. I didn't want anyone else involved. The less drama, the better.

My new motto: *keep my head down…uh, up and do my job.*

Fallon accomplished quite a bit before I arrived, and we finished everything with ten minutes to spare. Two glasses set on the counter, she nudged my shoulder. "Let's do a shot."

My scowl didn't hide my distaste. I leaned an elbow on the edge of the bar and considered her unwelcome request. For the first time all day I relaxed, thanks to her. When I had shared my male chauvinistic impressions, her wisecracking urged me on, putting me at ease and giving us a good laugh. "I'm not much of a drinker."

She snatched the tequila and wiggled it in my face. "Come on, I think after the day you had you need it. It'll help us get through the long night."

Her wagging eyebrows and pout made up my mind. "*Okay.*" Before I could finish my answer, she started pouring with flair, gliding up and down, then tossing and twirling the bottle before filling the next glass. Her technique could've taught the bartenders in the movie *Cocktail* a thing or two.

Drinks in hand, I prompted, "So, what should we toast to?" I hoped she had an idea because my mind drew a complete blank.

Fallon stared at me, her devious grin and mind formulating something good. "Hmm…"

The office door opened; both of us turned at the disturbance. Out strolled Linc and Sal, headed in our direction. They scooted onto the leather stools, positioned front and center. Sal's expression jovial. Linc's perturbed. He propped his arms on the bar and clasped his fingers together as he often did, sitting at his desk, relaxed but alert. "Good evening, ladies. We celebrating something?"

Fallon jumped in, answering in an overexcited and earsplitting voice. "Actually we are."

My full-to-the-brim glass held to hers mid-salute, I quirked my brow, no clue what she might blurt.

She winked at Sal. "A very *special* toast." Her glass clinked against mine, and she tilted it first at me and then toward Sal, announcing full of bravado, "To women who can change flat tires." She laughed and downed her drink, holding her gaze steady on a grinning Sal.

Funny, funny girl. I snickered and peeked at a scowling Linc before guzzling the clear liquid in one gulp. Proud I didn't upchuck afterward.

Linc snatched my glass and slid it across to Fallon. "Fill that up for me and get one for Sal. I have a toast too."

Uh oh. He had something cooking in that masterful mind. I set my chin in my hand and waited for the show. Business mode Linc could be best described as intense. A playful Linc—captivating. I couldn't take my eyes off him.

He waited as Fallon filled both glasses. His blue gaze never leaving mine.

Both men picked up their drinks, ready to salute. Linc turned to Sal, clinked glasses, and pitched, "To beautiful women who can do anything a man can do." Humor stretched wide across their faces. They knocked it back and slammed the empties on the bar.

Linc stood and palmed my neck, dragging my mouth to his for a sultry kiss. His temple on mine, he whispered against my parted lips, "See you after work. My place, okay?"

I nodded, my mouth scraping his in a dazed reply. He strutted across the room, greeting the eager clients. In the background I heard Fallon and Sal whoop with laughter and slap the bar, amused at their boss's blatant show. Lost in ecstasy my heart and body floated, reaching across the divide between Linc and me.

Fingers crossed, I prayed they didn't crash and burn.

Halfway through the night, the stock behind the bar dwindled. I took off for the storage room located in the notorious alcove. The difference, lights were installed and there wasn't a shadow in sight. I guessed Linc had something to do with that.

Wandering around for the bottles, I heard the door open and shut. Damn, this couldn't be happening again. I rounded the stacked full shelves and came to a halt at the entrance.

Jax was propped against the door with his arms crossed at his chest, a tattoo peeking out at the edge of his short sleeve T-shirt, and wearing black jeans that fit him way too well. Cool and composed, he lifted his chin at me, inspecting my body like a doctor who needed to perform surgery but didn't know where to start. If he didn't have such light blond hair, I would've pegged him for James Dean with that blatant, macho stance. This day just went in the shitter. "What are you doing in here?"

He sauntered over and stood so close, I could *feel* him. "I wanted to give you a hand."

Yeah, I bet he did. He had *that* look—sex on the brain.

"I can handle it, thanks." I took one step back and another while he stalked along, not missing a beat. I threw my hand out to his chest, halting his forward motion. "You should go. I've got this."

He picked up several strands of my hair and brought it to his nose. Before I could move away, he grabbed my upper arms and yanked me into his chest. "I want you." His lips grazed mine. About to tell him where he could go, the door crashed open, and there stood Linc with the most ferocious face I'd ever seen.

Damn, this alcove must be jinxed. Caught in a very compromising position I tried to step back, but Jax pulled me tighter to him, threw an arm over my shoulder and aligned me to his side like he wanted to showcase me to the world.

Oh hell!

"Linc, I need on the schedule for tonight," Jax said with a serious face, and my body stiffened at the implication.

He hadn't moved an inch, but his face went from ferocious to volcanic. "No."

Final answer. You'd think that would be enough, but no such luck.

"What the hell?" Jax spit out.

Linc marched forward and tossed Jax's hand from me, pulling me along with him. He looked back and barked, "She's off limits," and shoved me out the door.

I glanced back. Jax followed, but not too close. Linc pushed me forward the entire time. "Get back to work, Serena."

I stopped and glared at him. He looked pissed, no doubt about it, but I hadn't done a damn thing wrong. I was *doing* my "work" when I got interrupted. His knuckles ground into my lower back, urging me forward.

Great, just freaking great. "I'm *going…*" I said snidely, just as pissed, pointing behind us, inches from his nose. "You're gonna have to go back there and get what we need. We're low on vodka and whiskey." There, take that.

We stood there for endless minutes. When an intense man like Linc stared, it felt like an eternity. He leaned over, pushing his mouth so hard against my ear, his teeth scraped it as he demanded, loud enough to be heard over the music. "Final warning. Stay-away-from-Jax."

I did the same, but shriller than him. "My pleasure!" I stormed off and got my ass back to work—boss's orders.

Linc nowhere to be found when I finished work, I crashed in my apartment. Sometime in the middle of the night I felt a strong pressure on my back, and arms wrapped underneath me. Grogginess didn't disguise a thing. The contour of his body and his scent infused in every pore, he'd been branded on my brain for quite a while. So much so, that even in my sleepy state I *knew* Linc.

He whispered the same phrase three times, "I'm sorry, Serena," at my temple, in my ear, and when he tucked me against his chest, linking our hands together, he repeated the last one against my fingers.

I fell back asleep with a tiny smile and happier heart.

Chapter Fourteen

Three additional clients joined the ranks today. Once again they had a typical response, mentioning a friend of a friend recommended me. Numbers were my thing, and I gained a lot of experience at Gram's side, but in all the years we worked together, acquiring new clients in a steady stream wasn't typical. It could be luck or a fluke, I hadn't given it much thought before, but now, perhaps *someone* wasn't telling me something. There'd be only one way to find out. He should be in his office this time of day.

An empty lounge felt weird without loud tunes and gyrating bodies. A sense of déjà vu hit me as I approached a semi-open door. Instead of going in, I turned to leave, coming to a stop when I heard my name, said as if someone talked *about* me, not *to* me. I should've left but my curiosity wouldn't let me. Tucked along the wall, I listened.

Please forgive me for being so nosy.

"I'll triple the rate. In fact, I want a long-term arrangement with Serena."

Hell, it's Jax again.

"I told you she's off limits. She's exclusive already."

You tell him, Linc. I pumped my fist at my side.

"With who?"

"Me."

Yes, put him in his place—outta here, sucker!

"What are you doing, man? That's not like you."

Crap. Tell him, Linc. Tell him I'm yours and only yours.

"She needed a job, and I gave her one. It's temporary until she gets her finances together. It is what it is."

Bile tainted my tongue and a thundering brigade charged across my chest. I should've left, but I couldn't. It was like the people who witnessed a catastrophe and stood there— watching—doing nothing.

"So what's the big deal then? I'm a paying client."

Every bone in my body shattered and shriveled to the ground at the thought he'd turn me over to Jax.

"Don't. We're not going there. Not with her."

"Linc, I know you don't want to hear this, but I'll say it anyway because we're friends. We've been through hell together, so listen up. Think long and hard about what you're doing, and what it means. I'm guessing you haven't known her long. You have a lot going on and just as much on the line. Have you told her anything?"

"No."

"That's what I thought."

"You done, Jax?"

"For now…hey, I'm just watching out for your back."

"Yeah…yeah, I know."

I unglued my fractured body. Tears came in gusts and didn't stop for a long time.

My saving grace came in the form of a long walk to the mini-mart after the catastrophic eavesdropping. I bought three types of ice cream: Chunky Monkey, Cherry Garcia, and the pièce de résistance: Chocolate Therapy. Ben & Jerry's must have a psychologist on their payroll, because I could relate each of their flavors to an event and reason to eat them. Today's selections definitely related.

Arms full, I jabbed the elevator button. When it opened, I hurried in and imagined splendid and gigantic combinations. My goal: get to my apartment and eat until comatose.

One floor up the elevator came to an abrupt stop, the doors opened, and in walked B.B. Yikes! Slumped in the corner from the emotionally draining morning, I imagined my position sent an ill-intended message. Her squinty eyes and crooked smirk spoke volumes. I shifted my stance and kept my mouth shut, staring at the air vent above my head. Negative vibes wafted off her in waves. I couldn't deal with another mental slap. Not now anyway. My shitty mood rubbing against hers would be worse than grinding a million sticks of TNT together.

Weapons of mass destruction—total disaster and complete devastation.

"I heard you got my message." Of course she would speak first—the instigator.

Not sure what she was talking about, I ran through my memory banks for any instance but drew a complete blank. "What's that?"

Her belly laugh blasted my eardrums in the confined space. Since I had no clue, I remained quiet. She calmed herself pretty quick, realizing she hadn't gotten a rise out of me. "I heard you had a little problem with your car."

You got to be freaking kidding me! That bitch.

I eased up from my propped stance and stood to my full five eleven. In two huge steps, I stared her down with Wicked Witch of the West perfection. Fists firmed at my sides, I snapped, "I owe you one then."

"Oh, you owe me alright. Except, I think I'll take it with you on your knees…licking my shoes."

Gross. "You must not be too bright if you missed *my* message."

She snorted, her sing-song voice mocking, "What's that, *Saaadrena?*"

"It had something to do with…*a bloody face.* Since you didn't understand the first time, it looks like I'll have to make it harder and louder." Just as I leaned forward to grab her, the elevator doors opened. We both looked and there stood Jax.

Could this day get any worse? Yes! I needed to check my horoscope. The universe had to be in retrograde or spinning upside down, because this wackiness couldn't be explained by anything else.

His well-defined, veined hand held the door open. A *what the heck is going on?* expression and quirked brow pointed right at me, like I was the troublemaker.

Yeah, like I'd tell him anything. He needed to keep his own damn mouth shut.

I turned to B.B. and shot her a death-ray glare, communicating my silent and final warning. Snatching my bag, I stormed past Jax, leaving them behind to wallow in their demonic states together.

I hoped they speared each other with their pitchforks, annihilating one another in the process.

More than fuming and intent on expelling some of the negative energy, I hit up the best source of information—Mylaynee. Bowls filled to the brim with three types of icy goodness, we propped our feet up on wicker chairs, soaking up the afternoon rays out on the balcony.

"All right, I can tell something's buggin' you. What's up? You bought enough junk food to last a year."

I swirled the spoon through each scoop, mixing the flavors and spitting out the first of many questions. "What's the deal with Jax?"

She smiled wide and said with excitement, "Oh, did you get a chance to meet him?"

My pinched lips must have clued her in to the fact that I didn't share her enthusiasm. Her mouth turned down, and her disappointed tone said his bad boy side had been up to no good—again. "What he do?"

I burst out in laughter and at the same time tears rolled down my cheeks, almost as if a split-personality took over, and my psyche didn't know which persona to present first. Lost in my crazed thoughts, I paced back and forth and attempted to pull together the complaints I wanted to lodge.

"Hey." She stepped in front of me, grabbing my shoulders and halting my frantic movements. "Do you need me to beat the shit out of him for ya?"

That did it. My face dried and hysterical giggling won out, both of us unable to contain it. I wrapped my arms around her, calmed my ass down, and sat back in my seat. Ready to do what I intended when I came here—gather intel. I needed all the ammunition I could get, so I'd be better prepared to deal with Jax in the future.

"How do you know him?"

Again she smiled, tender rather than enthusiastic. "When I came here, I had a lot of bad stuff going on. He kinda adopted me." I lifted a brow at that statement. "Not that way, girl. I'm not his type. He's like a brother to me." My mouth dropped open; I could not believe it. She read my thoughts well and continued to protest. "Seriously, we aren't like that. We're good friends." She smacked me in the arm. "Get your mind outta the gutter. His company's in charge of security here. When his dad retired he took over the business. The guys he hires are all top-notch. You've seen them around, right?"

"Yeah, but I didn't know he had anything to do with it."

She nodded. "You met Sal, he's head honcho and manages them, but Jax is the boss. Linc contracts them. In fact, I work for Jax too."

"What?" I couldn't contain how loud it came out, and my previous shocked expression came back full force.

"Every once in a while, he asks for my help on cases. Linc doesn't mind, so I pitch in when I can. I like it." She shrugged and sat back down, taking a bite of ice cream. Hungrier than before, I picked up my bowl and dug in, even though it had turned mushy. "So you gonna tell me what he did to piss you off?"

Not sure I wanted the conversation focused on me right now, I remained fixed on my original target. "He's here every night. I mean, he's—"

Before I could finish, she cut me off. "If you're referring to his sexual appetite, yeah, you'll see him *all the time*," she rushed out, emphasizing the frequency and cementing an image of the bad boy engaged in hot and heavy deeds in the same breath. Dammit, I didn't want him in my head that way. "He's got tons of money to throw around. His gramps left him a trust fund he's intent on blowing on every girl in this place, except for me of course, and you," she clarified in a hurry.

Goodness, should I tell her about his full-blown efforts to get me in bed? I set my empty bowl down and glanced at her. She scooped them both up and yelled over her shoulder as she walked inside. "You want more to eat? I have some sushi in the fridge for lunch. We need healthy munchies to cancel out the bad calories."

It might help, so I agreed. I needed something good to cancel out—bad Jax.

Chapter Fifteen

Cement pounding below my feet, lungs huffing, head clearer than it had been in weeks, a five-mile jog had been the perfect way to start the day. Seagulls dashed into the bay, searching for their bounty. The whistling breeze, a perfect combination of warmth with a dash of cool felt wonderful against my sweaty flesh. The boardwalk this time on a Sunday morning included quite a few runners and bikers enjoying the shoreline. Most of them wearing headphones or earbuds, but not me. I loved every sound. The water, people, boats, everything. It calmed me. Regardless of what happened in my life, running had always helped set or reset the tone to a positive one. It had become a regular habit to spend at least a portion of my time outdoors.

Accepting this job five weeks ago brought a number of surprises—an angel—Mylaynee. After the amusement park outing, Miss Chatty Pants blabbed to the other servers about our excursion. From that moment on Paulette, Fallon, and Sage joined us. We hung out as much as possible. The Fab Five, as Mylaynee called us, were inseparable. It stuck and couldn't be a more perfect description of our combined personalities.

An activity Gram and I often did to "spread the sunshine" brought our group to the local children's hospital, reading, and making crafts, and just having fun with the kids. A nonverbal challenge commenced at that moment. The next week, Fallon decided we'd volunteer at the local homeless shelter. Mylaynee chose the "Best Buddies" organization, spending our day with disabled adults. Paulette wanted us to go to a nursing home. After I told her about the one Gram's girlfriends lived at, we ended up there. It had been a while since I'd visited, and having my new friends with me made it extra special. Sage chose the local animal shelter because she wanted to be a vet. Since she hadn't fulfilled that dream yet, she wanted us to contribute to their care in some way.

Sunday night became movie time. Choosing from Mylaynee's vast collection, we each threw one in a bag, and selected two. It caused a lot of razzing, but in the end added to the fun. Last week, Mylaynee announced our volunteer time would be known as "Sunshine Sundays" in honor of my gram. I bawled like a baby. Spending time with them had been an excellent ego boost. They were a dust-off-your-pants, get-back-out-there bunch. The only girlfriends I'd ever had, I cherished our time together. Beautiful women on the inside and out, they became my saving grace. Without them, I don't think I would've gotten through the disastrous B.B. incidents.

Linc continued to disappear on our days off. Most of the time I didn't see him again until Monday evenings. My heart told me one thing, my mind another, and my body screamed directives that screwed them both up. He spent the other nights with me, however nothing progressed any further. B.B. could be why he kept his distance. I had a strange feeling though, intuition maybe, that something else was going on with him. I could ask, but my conflicting feelings, along with risking getting fired and losing a hefty income, kept me in reserve mode. Holding it all inside created gut-wrenching tension. Add in to the mix, the conversation I overheard between Linc and Jax weeks ago produced another wake up call. I kept readjusting, reminding myself of my goals. It became a daily mantra, and if anyone heard me chanting *stay focused, don't let anyone get in your way, you can do it* every morning in the mirror, they'd die from laughter.

When difficult times hit, it amazed me where strength came from. Determined to do what I needed to, I garnered support from multiple places. Paychecks continued to roll in. Creditors were happy and my "in the red" debt ratio got smaller each week. Granted, I had a long way to go, but the strides I made served as a pick-me-up too. Bartending until wee hours of the morning didn't help with loss of sleep, but the enjoyment I got from watching and playing with the Millers' kids made up for it. Bookkeeping always rejuvenated me. It kept memories of Gram at the forefront and preoccupied the remainder of my daylight hours. It didn't matter how busy I got, I loved working. Less time to worry about other things that would only upset me.

Monique had finished renovating my apartment. All new furnishings indoors, including a luxurious lounge set for the balcony. Bamboo flooring throughout and sea-green walls gave it a serene feel. Decorative knick-knacks, a combination of antiques and contemporary pieces, embodied my style perfectly, even though I had no idea what it was myself. She created a harmonious balance, including pieces of furniture similar to the ones I grew up with and modern selections that suited my personality, making the place feel like home. She even made sure I got a cushy couch like Linc's. Any free second, I had my butt on it with a book in hand.

Now though, relief came in the form of a 5K. Two steps at a time, I barreled up the back stairwell. The last stretch before I fell into a cold and refreshing shower. Not a foot from my door and it burst open, my heart lodging in my throat.

Decked out in a Vera Bradley floral sarong she'd purchased on one of our jaunts last week, Mylaynee had a glorious smile stretched ear to ear. Her eager palms rubbing told me she was up to no good. What the heck?

"I've been waiting two hours for you." Her smile vanished as she glanced at her Brighton bracelet watch. Another recent buy.

Palms pressed to my knees, I sucked down massive gulps of air, attempting to recover from the jaunting three-story dash. Dang it, if I didn't love her to death, I'd bulldoze over her to get some water. Soaked head to toe, I needed relief and quick, but she stood sentry at my door. Her hip-holding posture and narrowed eyes cast a miffed attitude at me.

"Did I forget something?" I expelled each word on a short breath, inhaling and exhaling faster than normal. Damn, I'd pushed it hard, punishing my body on purpose. It worked too, easing my twisting emotions. Until now.

Her foot tap, tap, tapping and crossed arms answered me. When I glanced up, Mylaynee swung my apartment door shut and leaned her back against it.

What in the world was going on?

I straightened up from my bent position and waved my hand back and forth. "Are you gonna move so I can get in there?"

All of a sudden Mylaynee's smile returned, followed in quick succession with three raps on the door. I stepped forward while she moved backward, opening it.

"Happy birthday, Serena!" Paulette held at least a half-dozen-balloon bouquet, containing various exclamations. Sage tilted forward a sheet cake with vibrant turquoise, gold, and lime-green icing and well wishes on top. Fallon, arms full of decorative foil gift bags and wrapped boxes. Mylaynee wrapped an arm around my back, squeezing my hip, and pecked me on the cheek, calling out, "Surprise."

Particular moments reminded me of life's blessings: love, friendship, and selfless acts. They transcended words and renewed a person's spirit. Consumed in so many other things, I'd forgotten today's date. Heart alight, I placed a quick kiss to Mylaynee's temple, careful not to cover her in my sweat. The gesture repeated on the cheer line awaiting my regards.

After I took a quick shower, we piled into Paulette's car and ventured into New York City to one of the many spas. Another treat the girls planned. It turned out to be a relaxing event, complete with a hot stone massage, EmerginC facial, Moroccan rose organic body scrub, Argan manicure and pedicure, and a Samadi healing ceremony. A holistic, naturalist approach that had Mylaynee stamped all over it.

Peace and serenity infused in every fiber of my being.

Exactly what I needed.

Gifts unwrapped, half a cake gone, and on our second flick, we vegetated on any available surface in Mylaynee's apartment. Sage pegged it as Classic Film Night. Tonight for our viewing pleasure, *On the Waterfront* with Marlon Brando and *Some Like it Hot* with Marilyn Monroe. A huge Brando fan, Mylaynee got lucky when her choice was selected, and the one I picked with Marilyn also made it. Who didn't love Monroe?

Our snacks expanded too. Popcorn now included Goober chocolates. Paulette's contribution and concoction—the bomb!

Before I realized it, the screen credits had rolled by and the cleaning commenced. Paulette, Sage, and Fallon bid good night while I stayed behind, reluctant to return to my empty apartment. Mylaynee washed dishes, and I dried. "You heard from him?"

Crap. How did I know she'd go there? I mumbled, "Nope."

She handed me a dish and prompted, "Did he do anything for your birthday?"

I stacked the dried plates and cups in the cabinet and shrugged at the long shot. "It wasn't on my mind, so I doubt he knew."

Silverware in hand, she rinsed and questioned, "Have you asked him what's going on yet?"

"I'm afraid to. My heart might not be able to take it." I dried my hands on a towel and passed it to her. We finished in the kitchen and settled on the couch, continuing the heart-to-heart.

"I'm embarrassed to tell you this." After a pause that seemed an eternity I confessed, "We haven't had sex. I think it's because he's with B.B." Mylaynee shook her head, but I was on a roll and couldn't stop expelling my pent-up frustration. My face buried in my hands, I muttered, "What's he doing with me?" Pieces of my heart scattered everywhere, I gazed at her and pleaded, "*To me?*" She reached out, but I got up and paced in front of the TV. "I don't know what I'm doing. Have no clue how to handle a man like him." I flicked through a few DVD cases, pretending to study them. As I picked up the next one, her hand pressed on top of mine and pulled me into a comforting embrace.

I took a few steps back, but held onto her arms, unearthing my painful past for the first time. "Do you know what it's like not to be wanted? My mother didn't. She left me after birth. Twenty-two years and I've never met her." Her mouth dropped open. Not giving her a chance to interrupt, my explanation turned heartfelt. "Gram took me in. Filled my life with love and acceptance in more ways than one. But something happened—" I choked on the rest.

Returning to the couch, I tucked my legs up, wrapping my arms around them in a protective ball. She joined me, rubbing my back in a soothing way. I stared at the door and attempted to gather my overwrought thoughts. "My grandmother was the sweetest, kindest person you could ever meet. It didn't matter who you were. If you came to her and asked for anything, she'd give it to you without question. And she loved to cook and bake. We always did that together. She taught me so much." A thousand images of her flashed in my mind in a colorful kaleidoscope.

"But there's—a void." My chest constricted and in the next breath, I expelled with vehemence. "Not for my mother." I laid my hand on my heart and expressed with passionate conviction. "For *someone* right here." Her eyes filled with tears. She took hold of the same hand and wove our fingers together.

"Linc and I don't know each other well, but there's something there. I can *feel* it." My head pounding, I dropped it along the back of the couch and whispered, "Do you believe in fate?"

She nodded with a tender smile, almost like she'd gotten lost in thought herself.

"Me too," I crooned.

Her hand squeezed mine, and with the other she wiped her eyes. "Your friendship means so much to me. I love that you're here, Serena." She nudged my shoulder with hers. "You're my girl, right?"

I wrapped my arms around her ribs and hugged the stuffing out of her. Her support meant the world to me, and in one fell swoop she wiped out the loneliness I'd felt prior to moving here.

This day and my treasured friends—forever engraved on my heart.

Back in my apartment, I washed my face and brushed my teeth, anticipating a deep sleep. I stepped a foot in the bedroom and came to a standstill. Linc was sprawled on my bed, arms behind his head, ankles crossed, bearing a dimpled grin. His all-consuming presence filled the room with a sense of anticipation.

"W-what are you doing here?" I sputtered.

He dropped his feet on the floor and ambled toward me, grasping my hands and dragging me along as he walked backward. My stunned body plunked down on the comforter. He reached under the bed, pulled out a box with a humungous red bow on top, and plopped it on my lap.

"What's that?" Again, my response came out, making little sense.

His hardy chuckle charged the room with a potent zing. I closed my eyes and let the positive energy revive me.

"I've been waiting for you to get back so I could give this to you."

That statement had my eyes popping open. I wanted to remind him I'd been waiting a lot longer, but his expectant look kept the words locked inside. Instead, I glanced down and tried to figure out what he bought me. Would he get me lingerie? Nah. The large size canceled out jewelry. Besides, he wouldn't get me something like that. Could it be—

He grabbed each side of my head and tilted it up to him. "Serena, open it already." Not letting me guess anymore, he lifted my hand and plunked it onto the bow, crushing it. "What's the matter, you don't like surprises?"

Ha, if he only knew. I'd had more than my share. Just not enough of the good kind.

Seated next to me, he seemed more eager than a kid on Christmas morning. His body pressed against mine, buzzing like a live wire. The excitement got to me too, and I whipped off the ribbon and flung open the lid. Tissue paper thrown aside, I revealed the contents.

The silk, jade-green robe had a luxurious appearance, and the fabric was softer than any other I'd felt. When I glanced up, his scrunched brow and tight lips portrayed a side I hadn't seen on him often. "It's beautiful."

At my acknowledgement, a full-wattage smile transformed his face from intense to adorable in the blink of an eye. He took the gift from my hands and turned it around to the back. A variegated gold and orange dragon was embroidered on it, stretching from top to bottom. Fire shooting from its large-toothed mouth and red flames swirling along each shoulder. A bold, imposing figure balancing on a crystal ball that had a familiar quote with the identical Welsh characters stitched inside.

I skimmed my fingers over the stunning design. "You had that made...for me?"

"Try it on." He coaxed me over to a full-length mirror in my closet. While he stood behind me, he adjusted it on my shoulders and spun me around.

His bright, beaming face projected such awe, it caused my heart to lodge in my throat, making my voice wobbly. "Thank you." Clearing it, my bolder and unwavering gratitude showed my appreciation. "I love it."

"You sure? Liza will take it back." His hand took hold of mine, a gentle squeeze punctuating the claim with reassurance.

I chuckled and his brows scrunched. "My tattoo's on it. Who would want it?"

He wrapped his large arms around me, announcing, "She'd make you something else if I asked." Sure his request would be followed without a doubt.

I laid my head on his shoulder and basked in the moment. Unbelievable, the first man to enter my life owned an escort business. His kindness and generosity contrasted with the continued distance he placed between us, and made this whole situation surreal.

What was fate trying to tell me by throwing us together? It would be so easy to fall for him. Unable to predict the future, I couldn't determine how it would play out, but something told me to keep trying. To be patient.

He stepped away and glanced at his watch. "I have to go. I'll be back…later."

An internal sigh rumbled in my gut. Almost midnight, it didn't take much to figure out where he might be headed. Another reality check. The message loud and clear—booty-call.

Chapter Sixteen

Mylaynee sent me a text, saying she bought me a dress and wanted me to wear it tonight. The signature gold Forté garment bag couldn't be missed. I unzipped it and almost fell on the floor at the stunning, red-braided dress. It reminded me of the one I considered buying for the "interview," but instead decided on the white crochet. There wouldn't be a virginal appearance this time. *Lethal*—more like it. I slipped it on and turned to the full-length mirror. That girl was totally trying to get me laid—gotta love her!

The length hit about a centimeter below my crotch, and my boobs sported a definite increase by a cup or two, plumped up and screaming, *suck me, baby*. It might be a bad idea to wear this with sex-crazed men everywhere, but I felt wicked tonight. I threw on a pair of stilettos—bam!

Eat your heart out. Who's the bombshell now?

I turned the key, locking my door just as Jax came out from across the hall with a plastered, someone-got-lucky grin. Huh, looked like B.B. struck again. Or maybe Tanya. Heck, with him, it could be both.

Me + this dress = Did. Not. Care.

"Hello, Serena," he greeted with a sickening, tantalizing sex voice, still reeling from the after effects of his adventure no doubt.

Avoidance my best weapon at the moment, I spoke to the empty hallway in front of me and dashed toward the elevator. "Jax." I glanced back. Crap, right on my tail, his eyes glued to my ass.

Message to brain—do not let Mylaynee pick out your clothes.

I rammed the up button at least five times, yet it hadn't produced the easy out I'd hoped for. Instead it got me a chest glued to my back, with nowhere to escape. I turned around. "Going up?" I said, trying a lame diversion tactic and pretty much at a loss when it came to this guy. Linc wanted me to stay away, but it wasn't easy when he lurked around, hunting for his next conquest.

The rules must not apply to B.B. or Jax, because client "meetings" were supposed to take place in private rooms on the top floor, yet there he stood, so obvious he just had sex. A sweaty scent rolled off him in waves.

He reached up and twirled a strand of my hair around his finger.

"Don't," I reprimanded in my best authoritarian strict voice.

He dropped his hand, and his smooth, dreamy face morphed to stiff and calculating. "I saw you jogging the other day. How about I *come* with you some time?" Emphasis on the act he wanted caused my spine to snap ramrod straight. His musky scent choking me. I stepped to the side and as far away as I could get in the corner he had me pinned in.

Time to nip this in the bud and send him on his way. "Jax, there are plenty of girls here that would be happy to spend time with you. I'm not one of them." Well executed, if I didn't say so myself. Firm and to the point.

"Why not?"

Dang, maybe I patted myself on the back too soon. "I'm exclusive." That should do it.

"For how long?" The immediate reply and smugness hit their mark, serving as a hard reminder of the temporary state of my job and status here. My frown contorted to a scowl. Every one of my muscles wound tight—numb—kept me from returning a witty comeback. Jax and B.B.'s warnings ping-ponged in my brain, stabbing me in the heart over and over.

"It's time for a change," he declared in a confident tone, entering the elevator I hadn't even noticed had arrived. "Going up?" He repeated my earlier question in a sugary tone that grated on my every nerve.

I shook my head no.

The door slammed shut in my disheartened face, and sealed a whole lot more.

❧

Drinks served to one nameless face after another, the time passed without remembering a single moment. No, that wasn't right. I remembered something or *someone.*

Jax had been there all night but kept his distance. The women were all over him. You'd think it would've kept him distracted, but any time I glanced up, he always had those darn

Husky dog eyes on me. His presence was hell on my nerves, and his famous last words insisting "changes" were imminent put me in a tailspin.

Linc had been there too, off doing his job. He strutted around talking with one client or another, oblivious to my inner turmoil. It didn't make the night any better. At one point he came over and told me to meet him at his apartment when I finished. Stuck with my head *way* up my ass, I agreed.

As the evening went on, I watched him stroll about like he hadn't a care in the world. One beautiful woman after another stalked, caroused, and trailed him. He smirked and carried on a conversation without any regard to my feelings.

That flipped the switch—all-the-way-up.

My hand raised and ready to knock, the door flew open.

Mr. Heartbreaker stood there, as fine as ever in his custom-made suit.

"Get your ass in here," Linc roared.

Mr. Wrong-night-for-that! Microburst Serena swooshed in, twisting out of control and facing him head on.

He slammed the door and had the nerve to scowl at *me*. "What the hell is your problem?" His question reverberated as if he shouted it through a megaphone held right against my ear.

Tsk. Tsk. Wrong again.

My jerky arms whipped about, flapping up and down at my sides in blind and crazed misdirection. I stomped up to the hulking giant and stuck my finger like a well-honed pointer right at his heart.

"One." Stab, punctuating each word as I yelled them.

"You." Stab.

"Two" Stab.

"B.B." Stab.

"Three." Stab.

"Sundays." Stab.

With a parting flick to his chin, I whirled to the other side of the room, wrapped my arms around my aching stomach, and glared at the blurry harbor as tears flooded my eyes. Pent-up frustration never turned out well, often resulting in epic explosions. My temple pressed to the cool window, I waited for his reaction. An eerie silence engulfed the room, and it dawned on me that my uncontrolled rant might have dire consequences. He'd fire me for sure.

Clanking glass caused my high-strung body to jerk, slamming my shoulder into the wall. I whipped around and caught Mr. I'll-Just-Have-a-Casual-Drink, standing behind a bar in the corner. His silence and indifference as he sipped from the glass ratcheted another fire in my belly. Not missing a beat, his intense scrutiny remained in a standoff with my obvious fury.

"What do you want from me?" His response rolled over me and sweltered.

"I could ask you the same thing—sleep next to me every night—*naked*—not good enough for you—*sex tease*."

He slammed back two more shots before he countered, "What's your *real* question, Serena?"

Damn, his sarcastic remark and the tension brewing for so long over-circuited my brain, blowing my fuse. My live-wired, zapping heart charged in, taking over my mouth.

"Do you have feelings for me, Linc? *Feel anything at all?*

"You know what? Cra-zy! That's what I am." I yelled, shaking my head. "I should leave you, this place. Life out there…" I pointed toward the window. "Smacked me down lots, but at least I didn't have to *see* it, *smell* it, *taste* it every-freaking-day. I could turn a blind eye or bury my head under the covers, but not *here*." My arm flung around the room like some lunatic racing to catch a fleeing cab.

The glass perched at his lips slipped from his hand during my tirade. Brownish liquid splashed everywhere, the tumbler bounced off the bar and onto the wood floor, sounding like golf ball-sized hail raining down.

He stalked across the room, halting a mere inch from me.

My breath seized at the heated look on his face.

He swept his thumb in a soft brush across my cheek, drifting it along my neck and weaving his hand beneath my hair, holding the back of my head tight. At my hip, his other hand yanked me forward. Lips and teeth clashed together as he dove his tongue in, tossing mine around in a passionate, *you're not going anywhere* kiss. His peppermint taste and spicy cologne sucked me in. My hold loosened on his broad shoulders and began a descent. I took my time and let my hands explore each ridge on his chest and abs, drawing it out and ending up *way* lower. I grabbed his hard and thick shaft and squeezed.

He tore his mouth away from mine, swept me into his arms, and carried me to his bedroom.

Sprawled in the center of the comforter, I memorized every move he made. He undressed in slow motion, removing his shoes, socks, dress shirt, and suit pants. I hoped with all my might this would be our moment. *Please make love to me, Linc.*

At the foot of the bed, his stark nakedness caused my breath to stop. I wanted each gorgeous part of him captured in my mind and heart, so no details could ever be forgotten. It had been too long since I last saw him nude. Since the second night, when he asked me to undress him.

One after another, he edged his hands and knees along my body, like a panther marking his path and pursuing his next great hunt. His blazing blue, green, and black eyes studied my deer-in-the-headlights face, heaving chest, clenched hands, and trembling legs.

He lunged—to my neck—sucking, biting, dragging my flesh and feeding his ravenousness.

Yes, please, please take me.

Men shouldn't have such long hair. It was too tempting. Regardless, I threaded my fingers through the silkiness. A thousand strands fell along my shoulders, gliding over my skin like a masseuse's fingertips, stroking and caressing. I grabbed his neck and hauled his mouth to mine, devouring the million erotic flavors he embodied.

In seconds, he removed my miniscule dress, as well as the scraps beneath it, and aligned his hard and soft contrasting body on top of mine. Our moans echoed each other, radiating and trembling along my chest and stomach, and racing down to my scrunching toes. Between my legs, his warm and thick erection excited me so much that my inner sexpot took the lead. I shifted my body downward, positioning my opening above the tip of his shaft, inching my legs wider and wider and wider until—

He jerked his mouth away, bringing my covert maneuvers to an end.

"Make love to me." Hopefully my sincere plea didn't come across as desperate. Every day it got harder to not have him and to ignore him. My sexy dreams left me frustrated beyond belief.

His expression turned angelic. He pressed his lips to my temple and in a soft rasp said, "Someday, a special day, you'll have what you want. Your sweetness joining—" He took a long ragged breath and professed, "You're pure beauty, Serena. Making love will be something you will never, ever forget. It will steal your breath, your heart, and your soul."

There were horrible events that marked a person's life, never to be forgotten. On some obscure day, the memory would return, a reminder of that pivotal point in time— mind's cruel joke. Another sensory organism, the heart, joined in the misery. Together they wittily mocked, sending even the strongest individual into a never-ending spiral of doom and gloom. This was one of those instances and would haunt me forever.

What do you do when a man, who captures the essence of your being, says he doesn't want you in that way?

I pushed my face into the crook of his neck and inhaled long and deep. God, this man would be the death of me. My labored breathing wasn't the result of my nose being smashed against him, it came from humiliating disappointment. Either my virgin status or two-rating on the sexuality scale turned him off. On a daily basis, magnificence surrounded him, and foolishly I let myself forget that. The odd-ball in the mix and an Amazonian toad, my tall athletic frame with oceanic hips just got dumped in the reject pile. There wasn't any way I could compare to the exquisiteness that inhabited this place. At any time he could hand pick from the cream of the crop.

Beauty, indeed, was in the eye of the beholder.

So where did that leave me?

Yep, right here—between a rock and a hard place—Linc and nowhere to hide.

What I wouldn't give for a disappearing cloak or a time machine, giving me a chance to vanish. Since that wouldn't happen, I made every attempt to perform a sneaky removal from underneath him. I pushed and attempted to dash away, but he grabbed my arm, springing me back to the bed. Seated at the edge, I formulated another escape plan.

"Serena," he called, the deep, mellow tone sending shivers along my spine like a sad song.

I could not look at him.

The mirror told me what I would see—sympathy for a girl—now a woman who looked—*fill in the blank*. On any given day it varied, some good, some bad. I didn't hate myself. My evaluation came from a realistic view. I would always be an average-looking woman. Out in the real world, no problem.

This time, this place, this man = Not. Good. Enough.

He wrapped his arms across my bare stomach, holding me still. His hot breath and fiery naked chest engulfed my back, blistering the ice embodying me. *Ugh.* I closed my eyes, which forced other senses to take over. Accustomed to him, I recognized his Diesel cologne, a scent I liked a lot except right now. It caused my obsessive, washed-up emotions and head to spin. *Damn him.*

"Let me get dressed, Linc, *please.*"

He must have sensed my desperation or the pain in my voice, because he let go in an instant. I grabbed a shirt from the chair, covering what I could, and ducked into the bathroom.

I glanced in the mirror and told myself—*I will not cry, I will not cry.*

Famous last words.

Chapter Seventeen

Feet propped on a lounge chair, I concentrated on the rolling waves and boats far off in the distance. Were they coasting aimlessly or did they have some goal?

My purpose had been clear: pay off the debt. The progress had been consistent. Flourishing accounting business—*check*. Nanny job—*check*. Larger-than-ever paychecks and increasing tips—*check*.

The aimless part of my life—Linc.

His naked body and physical perfection could grace any artists' canvas. Painting nude forms made complete sense; some deserved the reverence. Even with his clothes on, the erotic images I had of him became a natural occurrence. Like an icon or idol, he got a lot of appreciation and every female lusted after him. I couldn't blame them. He exemplified a living, breathing sexual fantasy that few, if any, could ignore.

But—there were flaws too. Invisible to the naked eye and ones he hid well. If a person took the time to watch him *closely*, they'd see the hairline cracks behind his mask.

Wounds scattered—internal.

As much time as I spent examining his every move, I witnessed the haunted look appear, and just as quick, he'd recover, closing me out. Trying to decipher a complex man like Linc required finding a way "in," past his reserve and cautious lifestyle. The packed lounge evidence of his success and determination, and proof the business was his main priority.

Every day B.B. reminded me he belonged to her.

But I wanted him—beyond the physical.

Circumstances brought us together, and a pesky internal voice told me he'd be worth the risk. Even if my ego took a constant battering. Last night had been a prime example. After my crying jag, I came out of the bathroom exhausted to find Linc tucked into bed, concern etched into lines along his forehead. Nerves shot to hell from his blatant rejection, I climbed under the covers and scrunched myself onto the farthest tippy-edge of the mattress.

Instead of going to sleep, he embarked on an extensive twenty-questions session, inquiring about my life: growing up, Gram, work, anything and everything. From the day I moved in, he'd asked just one intrusive question—why I quit school. After that, he didn't pry any further. Perhaps, because he had a lot to protect too and didn't want to answer in return. A private person myself, I understood that well. Plus the ghosts in my own closet didn't need to be unearthed.

The pain I felt from our earlier interaction subsided the more interested he became in learning about me. As I responded, he'd twirl his fingers in my hair, gazing at the strands as they fell on my shoulders. When he tired of that motion, he entwined our fingers together, set them between our thrumming hearts and held them there as I talked. Before I realized it, the sun rose, and sleep came at dawn instead.

"Serena, where are you?" The urgent baritone yanked me into the present.

I turned around in my chair as Linc marched through the sliding glass doors, joining me outside.

"You ready to go?" he prompted with an attitude that said I should've prepared for departure and been out the door a long time ago.

"Uh, go where?"

"It's a surprise." His bright smile promised a good time. I, however, remained stuck in place, flabbergasted, since he'd never taken me anywhere before.

"What kind?"

He exhaled a long tiresome breath as if I were four years old asking, "Are we there yet?" Seated next to me on the lounge chair, he propped his arms across his grey T-shirt like I should've followed his command already.

My eyes had a mind of their own, embarking on a solo trip, bypassing his stern face and zeroing in on his bulging muscles, smack dab in the front of my nose.

He placed a thumb under my chin, directing my wayward gaze up to his twinkling blue eyes. The crook of his mouth tilting up a tad.

Dang, he caught me. I smacked his hand away. "Where we goin'?" My mood and tone sent a *don't mess with me* warning. If he thought he could yank me around, when I got done with him, he'd beg for mercy.

No sooner had the question left my mouth, Linc tossed me over his shoulder. Suspended upside down, I face-planted right on his ass. "What the heck are you doin'?" My hands clutched the humungous pockets on his cargo shorts, and I steadied myself. All the blood flowed to my head and stung like an ice cream brain freeze.

His hyena laughter continued as he exited my apartment, carried me into the elevator, and through the garage. All the while I had the benefit of admiring his—assets.

Aw, too bad, so sad for me. I might've even rubbed the plump, firm cheeks a teensy bit with my thumbs and fingers. Hehe.

Set on my unsteady feet in front of a super-bad-ass, black muscle car with white racing stripes down the center, a pounding head rush came on, making me woozy. I gripped his upper arms, hoping I wouldn't fall over. He bent at the knees and looked me square in the eyes. "I promise, it'll be worth the wait. I'm about to make one of your dreams come true."

Oh yeah? He could've done that last night, but *no*.

My inner-sass couldn't be contained. I launched a quick-fire retort that came with an over-exaggerated head shake. "I don't know, you've been havin'…issues satisfying me." His narrowed expression said he got the underlying meaning.

He yanked me against his well-sculpted form, nipping my earlobe and following it with a gruff counter. "Is that a challenge, Serena? Because you already know I'm a very determined man. I promise you, my performance isn't an *issue*, but exactly what you need."

Huh? What was that supposed to mean?

My curiosity grew to epic proportions during the drive. Without any further elaboration about his parting claim or where we were going, I became more and more perturbed. Sassy attitude upped a hundred percent, I crossed my arms along my chest and aimed my scrunched up tight nose and best snotty face toward my target—Linc. One-battleship…two-battleship…all the way to fifty-battleship. Damn, he didn't even clue in to my displeasure. His stare remained fixed on the road, not once glancing my way. The man had balls of steel, in more ways than one.

Okay, next strategy. I inhaled and exhaled real loud, sighing once, twice, three times while watching the passing scenery.

No response. Still ignoring me.

At the very least I wanted to know where we were going. The other perplexing message would have to wait, for now. Another strategy formed, I stomped my foot on the plastic floor board and continued to huff, acting like a four-year-old, and I couldn't care less. His cool demeanor and constant yin-yang annoyed the shit out of me.

I peeked at him several times, and it was apparent he'd remained unaffected by my actions. His silent lip-syncing to the soft jazzy tune playing on the radio and carefree attitude should've been reassuring. *Not.* My foot stomping slowed to a *rap tap tap,* and my huffing, although not as frequent, still sounded loud in the tight space. He had to hear me.

Okay, maybe more movement, something that would for sure capture his attention. I tossed my body to the window and then back real fast, glaring when I faced him. Regardless of my moves, he remained focused straight ahead, his thumb tapping on the steering wheel to the music. Six inches separated us, so he had to see me. I gazed out the window at the homes as they passed and reconsidered my tactics.

At that moment, his fingers crept up and down my waist. I twisted around in my seat and glanced down. Since I wore a halter top, my tan ribs were easy access for his wandering hands, which increased in pressure and vigor. "Linc, that *tickles*." I squirmed and shifted closer to the door, presenting my back to him. Hmph.

He tugged on my pigtails, flicking them multiple times, back and forth over my bare shoulder. As he repeated the act on the next pass, I grabbed his arm. "Stop it. What are you, *four*?"

I know…pot calling kettle black.

His cocky comeback—a wink, followed by straight and narrow concentration on the rural road.

I turned my back to him again, but that resulted in a pinch to my thigh. Daisy Duke- inspired short-shorts weren't something I'd wear, but they were a birthday gift from Fallon, which got them out of the box and on me for the first time. Without much room, my long legs couldn't be moved all that far away. I attempted to scoot them out of his reach anyway.

The swerving car catapulted me against the door. I threw both arms out and clutched the dashboard, glaring over my shoulder at the man and the maneuver landing us on the side of the road. He threw the stick shift into park, unlocked my seat belt, and latched his big paws onto my upper arms, hauling me across the center console. My legs widened and

straddled his lap as he lunged, mashing his mouth onto mine.
Our tongues joined in on the wild ride, mating in a wanton
kiss, fueled in part by the unfulfilled naked romps my body
had tired of.

He dragged his lips away from mine at a bewildering slow
pace, licking along my collarbone, trailing crosswise up my
neck, and flicking the outer rim of my ear, tickling it. Between
his hot and heavy inhales and exhales, he whispered not-so-
sweet-nothings. "Serena…" Tongue flick. "No way…" Flick.
"Not telling." He added one more parting flick and a smirk
that I felt on my earlobe, but couldn't see.

I bit down on his neck, my teeth clenching in a vise, and
providing a temporary payback for losing this particular battle
of wills. My overreaction could also be attributed to the
indecent sucks on my shoulder he reverted to when he finished
speaking.

Oh, I'd surrender, but not before I taught him women
always had the upper hand.

I leaned back along the steering wheel and jutted my thirty-
six B chest outward. His quirked brow issued a wordless
challenge, and his warm palms, flat on my bare thighs, injected
a fire into my bloodstream, urging me on. My plunging and
form-fitting halter top happened to be a godsend, hugging
every inch, and turning my boobs into a C-cup at least.

My devious plan began at first base, a seductive grin creased
my lips, and I licked them sensually up and down, biting the
bottom one. He leaned forward to kiss me but I shook my
head, and he stopped. Next, with my thumb and forefinger on
second base, I circled and pinched my nipples. His eyes

dropped, zeroing in on my breasts. At third base, I ground the crease of my Daisy Duke shorts into his crotch. He secured his hands on my hips, rotating his pelvis upward with each turn I made. Dang that felt good.

Concentrate, Serena. Time to make him suffer—crave me for a change.

On to the Grande Finale, I sucked a finger into my mouth, imitating a porn queen and issuing my best throaty moan, cranking my hips forward and pressing the center seam of my shorts on home base. I rubbed back and forth along his thick shaft, teasing and taunting him.

His grin stretched all the way to his forehead during my escapade, and his hands crept upward toward my nipples.

Oh yeah, I could win this round.

Diving across the console, I plopped in my seat and snapped the belt closed with a decisive click. My bull's-eye gloat met his open-mouthed gaze.

"Where we goin', Linc?"

His jolting laughter made his chest bulge out to an "Incredible Hulk" physique. He slung an arm over the steering wheel, reached across with his other hand, and pulled my palm up to his lips. In the center, he placed a kiss so tender and sweet that my toes, ankles, knees, and every other body part insisted it felt it too. His cornflower-blue eyes flicked up to mine, and he murmured a sultry concession. "You win." The insinuation could mean anything. Before I could decipher it and ask, he revved the engine, launching the car onto the road, and off we went.

I closed my eyes and relaxed against the headrest, smiling in anticipation of all the possibilities. Could his declaration mean he'd finally take the next step?

Rihanna's voice singing "What Now" competed with the wind humming through the lowered windows. Her lyrics were spot on, resembling my thoughts about this unexpected excursion.

What curveball would fate throw me this time?

Lake Fulton Marina, located thirty minutes north of Crestfallen, had boats of all sizes and types tied along the docks. Its shoreline had a tiny beach area on the other end, far away from the launch pads. Warm temperatures and a sun-filled afternoon urged many families to lounge on the sand and carouse in the water.

Linc pulled a picnic basket from the trunk, grabbed my hand, and walked us toward the wooden boardwalk.

"You have a boat here?"

"Yes."

"When'd you get it?"

"Hmm...'bout six years ago."

At last, a direct answer and teensy morsel about the elusive man.

"That's it." He pointed toward a sailboat, thirty or forty feet long, bobbing up and down with the current. His large body was closer to it, and I had to peek around him to read the sparkly maroon script on the stern.

"Serenity?" The question gurgled in my throat along with an imperceptible gasp. Prickles spread from the base of my neck to the roots of my hair, sending a shiver down to the tips of my toes and turning my legs to lead. I searched his face for a clue and waited for an explanation to the origin.

He shrugged and held out his palm to me, stepping one foot onto the boat deck, the uneven surface and rocking motion unnoticeable in his sturdy frame. Sure-footed and confident, he curled his fingers, urging me to come closer. I took hold of his firm grip, which provided the right balance for my long legs, adjusting to the height difference with ease.

Burnished wood trim against the white hull added a warmth and hominess. Any reluctance I had at the beginning of the excursion vanished at the glorious waterway awaiting me.

He motioned for me to take a seat, pointing toward a cushion at the back. As swift as the breeze, he tugged on lines and unwrapped cords, agile and effortless. Mundane work for some, his whistling tune and uncontained positive energy demonstrated he enjoyed the preparations.

Not long after, sails casting to and fro, we drifted further away from the marina.

Bright sunshine painted the sky a fluorescent blue. Birds' high-pitched squawks spread a message for all to hear. Followed in turn by sing-song tweets and twitters. Rolling waves slapped the hull and splashed sprinkles on my face, fixing like dew and refreshing my basking, overheated skin.

Captain Linc's impressive stature at the helm showcased his magnificence, amplified more so by the boat's undulations and the expansive sea as his backdrop. Curiosity about the boat's name not forgotten, I opened my mouth to ply an answer out of him, but he beat me to the punch. "Why'd you get that tattoo?"

Ah, so he must have found out what it meant. Interesting. Confident in the seclusion of our setting, my quip came out in a tit-for-tat, indicating he'd better be in a revealing mood. "You gonna tell me why you chose Serenity?"

Again, his shoulders jerked up and down. This time though, over the bustling wind he announced, "We're all searching for it." He pinned me in a direct stare. "Can you deny it?"

I tipped my face up to the heated sky, closed my eyes, and drew in the sea-scented breeze. A voice I knew well stirred internal, recalling the perceptive insight I had heard repeatedly and believed since childhood. "My grandmother used to say that destiny presents us with gifts of unlimited potential, offering us choices from a bountiful selection. Our actions dictate what happens in the future. Fate forewarns us though, by throwing obstacles in our way. Sometimes they're silent, other times they're obvious, and an attempt to steer us in a certain direction. If the path is right, it's confirmed in some way, affirming, 'Yes, this is the right way.' On occasion, because fate works on its own timetable we get impatient, and our efforts to move on are resisted, so we're slowed down, which is meant to warn us, 'Wait, not yet.' Then during the most difficult times of our life, there's an inner voice that holds all the answers, but it's often ignored. That, my gram says, is fate's soulful call whispering, 'I have something better planned for you.'"

"The path to serenity appears amid the storm." His reverent translation of my tattoo implied he believed in divine intervention too.

I nodded, wanting to acknowledge I'd heard him, but also because I agreed a hundred percent with the notion. Memories from the past clashed with the present, causing me to tear up. I turned so he wouldn't see them and watched the rippling waves.

Gram's inspirational expressions helped me when my mother's rejection got the best of me, or when peers didn't accept my wallflower status, or worst of all, when she was diagnosed with cancer. Hearing him recite the quote like she did many times brought back painful memories, but it also soothed, infusing me with her perpetual optimism too.

Linc dropped the anchor, bringing the boat to rest in a hidden cove. He set the wicker basket on a cushion beside me, flipping open the woven panels, and taking out clear glass plates, silverware, and beige cloth napkins. He reached in again and wiggled in my face multi-layered sandwiches, fruit and pasta salad, and giant frosted brownies.

"Did you make all that?" I elbowed him, tilting my head toward the feast.

"Absolutely." His toothy grin exposed the little white lie. I attempted to pick up a plate, but he swept my legs out from under me and hauled my butt onto his lap. As if he hadn't just performed a Superman feat, he recited the menu in a casual flair. "We have turkey and roasted peppers, ham and cheese, or veggie. Which do you want?"

Sun highlighted the fine age lines on his face and little green sparkles dotted the blue in his eyes, letting a vitality and brilliance shine through. His mask disappeared, gracing me with the "in" I desired. A wave rocking the boat jostled my brain, and I answered him. "Turkey, but I should sit over there," pointing to my original seat, "that way we have room to eat."

"No. Stay where you are." His order not harsh but soft and tender, his grip tightening instead. He prepared two plates with a little of everything, including a brownie for each of us. I reached for a turkey sandwich, but he picked it up before I could and brought it up to my mouth.

I looked at it and then at him. "I can feed myself. Give me that..." My lightning fast reach did no good, because he suspended his long arm well over my outstretched hand.

"Let me," he insisted, adding a puppy-dog pout.

"Linc," my warning started but died out. A vision of him flashed as a little boy, plump lower lip jutted out, demanding his way or else. His haunted disquiet nowhere in sight.

My mouth opened and with a constricted heart, I let the adorable man feed me lunch.

Chapter Eighteen

When we got back, I had just enough time to take a shower and get dressed for work. Hectic as usual, the mad pace at which I prepared drinks left no time for conversation beyond "What can I get you?" I turned to help the next customer and ended up head-on with Mr. Miller. You've got to be freaking kidding me.

"Serena, is that you?" He set his arm along the edge of the bar and leaned in real close. First, examining my face and then sliding to my breasts, which overflowed from the single-banded strap molded to them, covering my nipples, but exposing the top and bottom mounds. Another birthday gift.

Determined to do my job, I responded in a deadpan manner. "Yes. What can I get you?"

"You work here?" He flung his suit-clad arm around the room while speaking.

Taken aback by the obvious question, I replied in monotone and drawn out, "Uh…*yes*." It clicked then, why he was here, and my demeanor switched to snarky. "Drink, *Mr. Miller*?"

Face reddening, he stammered, "Umm…Uh…" In a jerky fashion, he peered around the room and must've figured out the repercussions of being seen at this club. "Look…is there somewhere we can talk *privately*?" he yelled over the music.

Just then, Linc appeared at Mr. Miller's side. "Is there a problem?" He glanced between us.

Mr. Miller took a few steps back, jutting his chin toward me, and said, "I need a few minutes alone with her."

"In my office, over there." Linc pointed across the lounge, motioning him forward. Without missing a beat, he turned toward me and directed, "Get Paulette to cover you and come join us, okay?"

I entered a few minutes later. Linc sat behind his desk, as usual a dominating presence. I plopped down in the chair next to Mr. Miller, crossing my arms and aiming a quirked brow at him.

"What exactly is your concern?" Linc's direct and to the point manner, although stated in a respectful and professional way, presented an air of no arguments.

Mr. Miller's dressed for success style and CFO status covered the part that got him access to this exclusive place. Yet his shifting shoulders and sweat dripping from his brow showed a lack of confidence in this situation. He pointed at me and declared, "She-she knows my wife."

Ha! He should have thought about that *before* coming here. Not that he knew I worked here, but still. Poor Mrs. Miller. She'd be crushed if she found out how he spent his free time.

Watchful and silent, I deferred the matter to the boss. No way in hell I'd speak now, because professional, nor respectful, would be in my vocabulary.

"As my employee she's bound to confidentiality. You received the invite, therefore, you're welcome to remain. However, if you choose to leave and not continue with the club's benefits, I expect the same in return. Do we understand one another?"

Mr. Miller's eyes closed tight, and when he reopened them his shoulders slumped, wiping out the last remaining bit of his executive stature and composure. "Yes. I understand, perfectly." He turned toward me, a noticeable tic in his eyelid. "Do I have your word you won't tell Nancy?"

Friggin' jerk. Not dignifying his question with a verbal response, I dipped my chin in confirmation, while in my mind I sneered and shot him full of daggers.

He extended a hand across the desk to Linc and left without a second glance at me.

Bound to erase the troubling encounter by drowning myself in work, I dashed toward the closed door.

"Serena." His concerned voice stopped me in my tracks.

It sucked that the day ended like this. The afternoon had been so wonderful. Linc came up behind me and administered an understanding and deep-penetrating massage across my shoulders, down my arms, to the tops of my hands, and around each finger, weaving his with mine. Cheek to cheek, he pressed his chest with assurance to my back. Lips brushing my temple he whispered, "You okay?" Hands still clutched together, he wrapped his arms across my stomach and consoled me with a gentle sway in sync to the beat playing in the adjoining room.

Determined to put it out of my mind, I changed the subject. "You did good today." I tilted my head back, so I could see him better, and clarified, "Sailing was amazing. Anytime you want to make my *dreams* come true, you have my approval." My cheeky grin and batting eyelashes punctuated the affirmation.

His same unfettered and unmasked presence I saw on our trip radiated in grand magnitude from him. The humdinger he delivered proved it. "Told ya—I'm *exactly* what you need, *issues* and all."

ॐ

Mrs. Miller didn't have to speak. My steps faltered at her flushed cheeks, moistened eyes, and catawampus mouth. Eight years working for this family dematerialized in seconds.

"You have to leave. I tried to call, but you didn't answer." Even with the kinked strands sticking out all over her messy bun, the full-guard mode she took at the front door contrasted with her despondent and frazzled persona.

"Please, can we can talk?" The more reasonable of the two, I hoped she'd at least grant me that.

She shot a distressed glance backward, and an instant later she stepped down from the brick porch, meeting me at the bottom. "Please, you have to go," she said with urgency. "I can't—we—I have to let you go." She clutched her upper arms. Her sigh and strained send-off lodged a lump in my throat at the finality. "You can't work here anymore." She dashed up the stairs and came to a stop at the door. Without turning around, the low and soft farewell reached me in the noiseless, early morning hour. "You'll be missed, Serena."

As she twisted the knob, the door flew open. Mr. Miller, fit to be tied, yelled, "Get in here now!" He snatched her arm and tossed her into the entryway, slamming the door behind her stumbling body. "Don't make me *escort* you off our property." Fury and disgust filled his tainted order. The higher-than-mighty executive on display failed to scorch the crud off his doorstep.

Pride swallowed, my shaky plea revealed a crushing disappointment. "Mr. Miller…Stan, I love your kids. Please, I'd hate for last n—"

"*Get-out!*" Barreling down the stairs, he came nose to nose, even though I scrambled backward, his harsh warning stalked me. "*Don't* open your mouth." The impending death threat clear.

I turned tail and sprinted the hell away.

Chains twisted from bottom to top, the swing sprung me in a twirl, compounding the dizziness already unsteadying me. Adult mallards guided ducklings in an effortless, casual glide across the pond. Robins and starlings hopped and flitted about, portraying a picture-perfect, carefree existence. If only my journey through life could be that simple.

Croton Point Park, a home away from home, had become a mandatory route and preferred place to exercise. Images of Gram's power-walking and rapid, pumping arms brought a brief smile to my not-so-happy face. The warm and sunny day should have been enjoyable, but my depressed, beat-up condition made it hard to delight in the serene setting.

Tainted thoughts battered me into a slouchy pulp. Mr. Miller's high moral ground and irrefutable stance, insinuating my influence could somehow corrupt his kids, made him a hypocrite. Either he thought I would tell his wife, or he thought my job involved—yeah, not going there.

I kicked my feet on the ground, shoving the swing back and forth. The motion didn't bring the soothing effect it used to. Instead, my insides twisted more and the gurgle in my stomach said it was time to go. I bent over, stretching my palms flat on the grass and bouncing on the balls of my feet a few times. Arms stretched above my head, I reached toward the sky, wiggling my fingers and rolling my shoulders, relieving a tiny bit of tension. Setting a pace that mimicked Gram's when she came along during my jogs, I took a detour onto Willow Street. Weeds and grass higher than my last visit, my longing gaze examined every square inch of my childhood home. Gram's spirit occupying my mind and heart.

Japanese maples surrounded the lot. Each included wooden bird feeders and houses I'd painted myself. Twenty-one for every birthday and as many as she could buy before her death. I should've wrapped them and taken them with me, but I couldn't. I didn't have the heart to remove them from their special resting place.

Two fingers sealed to my lips for a kiss, I extended it toward heaven in a wave.

I remember. Always. Forever.

Memories of her gentle smile, wheezy-whistling laugh, and sea-green eyes brought happiness to me and everyone she came in contact with. Her selfless acts were treasures she shared with each individual, offering affection and encouragement no matter the situation.

In a blur, my position changed from a Cape Cod house to a brick apartment building.

Home, for now.

Linc jumped up from the sofa, frowning as soon as I entered. "What's the matter?"

I shuffled over to him and dropped my head on his broad, supportive shoulder. "The Millers fired me." Disappointment evident in my mumble against his neck, my arms wound around his ribs for added consolation.

"Dammit, I'm so sorry," he murmured against my cheek, scooting me onto his lap and shielding me in a protective embrace. His awesome bear hug soothed the direct hit and gouging remarks remaining from the earlier altercation. "Want me to call Stan?"

"*No.*" My quick reply and stiff body must have clued him in to my discomfort. An instant image of Mr. Miller storming after me produced the knee-jerk reaction.

He shifted me back and examined my face. His narrowed eyes attempted to mind meld the truth out of me. "Did something else happen?" Although a question, his gruff tone and flexing muscles promised retribution. Ha! Second time today. The ominous technique must be taught in boy's-only classes.

Reluctant to cause more problems and ready to put it behind me, I told him a little white lie. "Nothing I couldn't handle." I glanced at a photo of Gram and back at him, willing an extreme calm into my voice. "I'm disappointed, that's all." Instead of indifferent, my lips trembled, and my overwrought body slumped against him, sure he'd support me and not let me fall.

Note to self: when depressed—don't consume Ben & Jerry's—devour a hunk of Linc. Low fat and does a body good.

Several minutes later, he dashed down the hall and came back holding a book out to me. "Read. I'll make you breakfast and we'll chill."

"Uh, don't you have work to do?"

He raised my palm and plunked the book in it. On my right side, he propped a couple pillows and swept my feet from the floor, sprawling them on the cushions. The swift out-of-the- blue move had me falling back and inclining flat. "Rest." He dashed into the kitchen, speedy-fast as Flash Gordon.

I cupped my hand at my temple and saluted his back. Aye, Aye Captain. No fuss. No muss. No arguing.

Rather than throwing myself into bookkeeping or chores, I let myself take a mental health day. Not that Linc would let me do otherwise.

After eating, he raided my bedroom closet and lugged an armful of board games into the living room, swindling me into playing the afternoon away. We razzed, elbowed, and wrestled each other through each wonderful, hilarious game. I watched with rapt attention as the bigger- than-life man sat Indian style and *played,* which would've left any woman with half a heart.

It was sad. He beat me in Monopoly, Clue, Yahtzee, *and* Scrabble, rubbing victory dances in my face after each loss. His gyrating, and butt and arm pumping, did me in. Warning labels should be slapped across his fantastic body. When he smiled deep from his soul, the happy-go-lucky appearance devastated me. Throw in his knee slapping, gut-wrenching laugh that radiated through his entire being—he took my breath away. My heart had no chance. I would not survive the devastation—bamboozled, all-out goner, head over heels.

It would've been nice to laugh along with him, but I couldn't. Not wanting to miss a single second, I sat in still silence with an admiring smile, mesmerized by his silliness.

And on some subconscious level, I desired to see him— *genuinely happy.*

Since the first day I met him, the melancholy he wore on a regular basis and an agonizing sensation called to me. Drew me like a moth to a flame. Not for the light—because of the pain, the burn. Two yearning souls—conversing in silence— unburdening each other's torment.

Whether he realized it or not, he had a tell that gave him away. At least *I* thought he did. Shadows would pass and shutter, causing his blue eyes, day or night, to become cloaked like a ghost. Now though, that look was nowhere to be found.

A couple hours before the lounge opened, Linc and I remained cuddled on the couch, watching—*game* shows of all things. Winner's choice. He had a serious obsession.

"Serena." His abrupt call-out had me searching his wrinkle-free face for a clue to the urgent plea. "Thank you. I had fun…kicking your ass." His beaming grin made his cheeks puff up like a chipmunk's and little crinkles appear in the corners of his twinkling blue eyes.

Oh, a lucky day for him indeed. In a great mood, I acted as if the smart-alecky comment didn't deserve an ass clobbering and nodded, not in agreement, but in confidence. Giving myself a mental pat on the back, I launched a casual, non-affected, chit-chatty comeback: "I let you win."

Just as the last syllable left my mouth, his rabid tickling began, causing me to leap to the floor and scramble away to an unnamed home base. *Game on!* The seven-inch height difference had me at a serious disadvantage. Tackled from behind, we tumbled and rolled like spinning tops, the inertia petering us out, until I lay flat on my back with Linc beside me in the exact same position. The ceiling twirled and our loud, huffing breaths echoed one another. Leftover grilled chicken and perspiration, an aroma that any other day would be a terrible combination, in one breath smelled like heaven.

He intertwined his sweaty palm with mine, his rhythmic pulse thumping on my wrist. Different than any other time before, but somehow the same, he brought my hand to his moist lips and graced one finger after another with a heartfelt, worshipping kiss.

From the corner of my eye, a single tear trickled into my ear, conveying in a private whisper a message of love and peace to its twin consoling soul—Linc.

Chapter Nineteen

On the interstate for over two hours, Linc turned the black SUV onto a windy road, each side bordered by towering weeping willows and creamy-white, blush-pink, and pale-blue flowering dogwoods. A breathtaking and picturesque scene provided a major motion picture view. A few miles along, a stone mansion similar to a castle from medieval times appeared. I leaned forward, almost pressing my nose to the windshield in wonder. Photographs and paintings couldn't come close to reality and the stunning grandeur.

Quiet the entire trip, he pulled into a parking spot near the front entrance. Anticipation and nervousness had me climbing out and onto the lush green lawn with a rainbow of blooming scents. Botanical gardens dotted the landscape left and right, including the entire foreground.

He led the way to a small portico made from rough-hewn rock and pushed an intercom button. Mahogany doors at least fifteen feet high with carved, angelic-like centerpieces added to the regal appearance.

"Yes, how may we help you?" the monotone voice called.

"Lincoln Jefferson."

No matter how many times I heard his name it gave me chills. Either his parents were politicians, or they had a thing for presidents. From head to toe, his tall stature and intense demeanor were well suited. A powerful and formidable man, it fit him *very* well.

At the buzz, Linc stood back, letting me enter first. Antique mahogany panels decorated the walls and thirty-foot-high ceilings, and included polished marble floors, the stately appearance enhanced by paintings and statuesque bronzes often seen in museums—fit for a royal family. Unbelievable.

A short, gray-haired woman with a beaming smile greeted, "Lincoln, it's wonderful to see you," extending her hand to him and turning to me with the same gesture.

"This is Serena," he relayed in a solemn tone, apprehension evident in his stiff form and fisted hand gnawing my lower back.

"I'm Mrs. Golden. It's a pleasure to meet you." Pleasant but reserved, she glanced between me and Linc several times throughout the brief introduction.

"Likewise." My whispered reply seemed necessary, since the tension rolling off Linc snapped onto me, shattering my vocal cords when I spoke. Suddenly, the unknown reason for this trip and turn-on-a-dime exchange induced a discomfited *this is not a happy occasion* premonition and life-altering anxiety.

"We're going up." He directed, not wasting any time, herding me in front of him and toward the stairs.

"Sure, of course, Lincoln. If you need anything let me know."

He nodded to her on the way up the grand staircase.

At the top, plush red carpeting and antique furnishings lined the hallway along with several closed mahogany doors. He stopped in front of the last one on the right, breathing deeply before his somber voice broke the silence. "Serena, thank you for not asking questions and… giving me time." The last few words trailing off on a hush.

Scared to death of his constricted face and the other side of that door, I wanted to cry, but couldn't figure out the reason. Gathering courage, my slight smile came out of nowhere.

His white-knuckle grip on the knob turned right, and he walked in first, his rigid shoulders in my direct line of sight, blocking the view.

Elegant furnishings and surroundings continued into a bedroom. My attention drawn, though, to the most stunning young woman I'd ever seen, worthy of gracing any fashion designer's runway in the world. Except her prone body, motionless in a bed, said my assessment wasn't quite right. The longer I watched and waited for her to wake up and acknowledge us, the more I began to notice about her, and determined this was a dismal scene. Colossal lumps clogged my throat while I stood still near the entryway, unable to move any further.

Linc sat in a cushioned chair near a large picture window, clasping his hand around the sleeping beauty's pale one. Moisture filled his eyes as he motioned for me to sit in the adjoining seat. "I brought Serena with me today." His graveled, heartbroken tone caused me to collapse with abrupt finality in the chair. My gaze flitting from him to the woman, a massive hole forming in my stomach and extending up to my chest, both constricted and burning.

He leaned down and kissed her hand with such love and tenderness, I had to turn away as tears flooded my eyes. "This is my sister, Belinda." His whispered greeting forced me to face him.

Oh, Linc. Not able to stop my own cascading tide, I grabbed hold of the armrests and prepared myself for whatever he might say next. He cuddled her fragile hand against his cheek, and as he blinked, one after another of his tears were captured on her fingertips. I wasn't even sure she could feel them, because she hadn't moved since we got here.

Her lean body clothed in an immaculate yellow organza dress appeared ready for a night on the town. Their resemblance uncanny, her midnight-black hair, lengthy frame, and beauty matched her brother's. Uncertain what to say, he must have sensed my reluctance and explained, "She's been here...almost ten years." He paused and on an exhale murmured, "She was in a coma, but now—PVS." His voice so faint, had I not been inches away I wouldn't have heard.

God, no. After experiencing Gram's sickness and seeing her body deteriorate, I understood the helplessness. But *this*, year after year willing a stagnant form—to wake—to live. Gut-wrenching pain consumed me, along with a deep affection for him and the never-ending agony her condition sentenced him to.

I brushed the wetness from my eyes and pulled a portion of his devoted strength inward before speaking. Even so my voice wobbled from the noticeable suffering. "What happened?"

A shake of his head brought any further discussion to an end. "Later, okay?"

In silent agreement, I placed my hand on top of his and his sister's, all three lying at her side.

ᕕᕗ

We spent two hours in the room while he told her about his week and the goings-on in the world. A way I guess to maintain some type of connection even if she couldn't return the sentiment.

Afterward, he and I walked along the floral-lined pathways, and I waited for him to speak. When he did, the entire tale gushed out, as if not wanting to ever repeat it again.

"She's three years younger. The age difference didn't mean a thing though. We spent every minute together. A week after I graduated high school our parents died in a car accident. Since she was underage, even though I was eighteen, the courts weren't sure about custody. We didn't have any other family, and eventually the judge decided in my favor.

"From the time I turned sixteen, I had a job. My parents taught me to be frugal and save, which helped afterwards. I had a full academic scholarship and college plans, but ended up not going. We were just two lost kids, whose lives would never be the same.

"I didn't know shit about bills and expenses, which made managing finances a hell of a lot worse. The insurance company didn't pay right away and added to the problems. The first year, I used savings to pay the mortgage, cars, and expenses. When the insurance did pay, it was enough to live on a while. None of that mattered though."

On a deep sigh his voice wavered as he described the resulting effects. "My sister…shit." He came to an abrupt stop and stared up at the sky, taking several gulps before he continued. "Losing them both that quick hit her hard."

He grabbed my hand in his and turned toward me. "I tried—I tried so damn hard to help her. Working two jobs, I wasn't home much. She needed more than a fucking paycheck…needed a brother…needed attention…needed…" He turned away from me, his mumbles filling the space between us. "Caught up in my own shit I didn't realize…"

My heart hurt at the self-defeat in his account and the trauma they had both experienced. After a moment, I laid a reassuring hand on his shoulder. A small gesture and nowhere near the engulfing embrace I wanted to give. To capture and wipe away every ounce of his pain.

Cuddled up to his side, I held on to his arm, leaning in to offer unspoken support. His face looked light years away. "A year later, a few months before her eighteenth birthday, I came home and found her beaten to a pulp." His hand squashed mine like a vise, but he didn't seem to notice. Pinpointed on the landscape, his gaze *really far off*, reliving a nightmare stuck on rewind.

"The police told me a few weeks later, when they arrested a pimp for her assault, that my sister was a prostitute. It was her punishment for a job gone wrong." Head down, his next testament transformed his typical strength to debilitated in mere seconds. "I didn't even know." His deep voice cracked when he continued. "Belinda's in a permanent vegetative state. Doctors say she'll be that way until—" he drew in a ragged breath and expelled, "as long as she lives."

He spun around and cupped my cheeks, his solemn eyes holding mine. "I come here *every* Sunday to be with her, any way I can, all day and night."

I placed my hand on his and attempted to school my thoughts. "After everything that happened—" Trying to form a delicate response that didn't sound insensitive, I glanced away and figured out what to say before looking at him again. "Why do you own the lounge?"

He examined my face and a firm, committed response accompanied it. "I do it *because* of her. For whatever reason women choose this business, I don't want them strolling the streets having some asshole controlling every move, taking their money, or worse beating them to death. At my place, *they* decide and don't have to do a damn thing they're not comfortable with. The clients pay a hefty fee for the privilege and every penny goes in their hand. I don't take a fucking percent. Which wouldn't happen anywhere else and you know it. My living is made from the building leases, bar, and other businesses I invested in over the years. After what happened to her, I had to *do* something."

I diverted my eyes, focusing on a white trellis covered with climbing purple roses, and considered what he said. In some ways his decisions were logical, stemming from unfortunate circumstances. My own reasons for entering this business were selfish, driven entirely by money. When presented with an injustice he took direct aim, altering his own life after a tragedy struck his one remaining family member.

How many people would go to such an extreme?

I positioned my hands on his cheeks, gathering him closer, chest to chest. Questioning blue eyes lightened even more by the sun shining on his face held me focused as I spoke with complete assurance and from a fulfilled heart.

"I love you."

In a trance, and unlike his usual calm and cool demeanor, he stammered, "W-what did you say?"

Extended on tiptoes, I wrapped my arms around his neck and pressed my mouth to his, guaranteeing with consummate conviction. "I-love-you, Lincoln Jefferson."

Every wrinkle on his tense face disappeared in a flash and the unforgiving weight he seemed to always carry on his thick shoulders vanished.

Locked in each other's embrace, the fathomless, soul-bearing kiss he bestowed on me resembled a touch used for a priceless treasure—precious.

Chapter Twenty

The pathway and scenery changed from cobblestone to pea gravel and grass to dirt. A light breeze perfumed the air with honeysuckle, jasmine, lavender, and many unknown sweet fragrances. Linc's long stride marched at breakneck speed, intent on a location he refused to divulge. For some reason I didn't argue and paraded along, enjoying the view while he tugged me from behind.

Oak, pine, cherry trees, and giant ferns surrounded our entry into the woods. Fixated on my feet, I skirted over little ruts and around big divots. Linc didn't have any problems though. Without hesitation he darted around trees and over logs. Thistles and sharp stalks scraped my ankles as the path narrowed. When we crested a small knoll, a sudden chill brushed over my skin. Thick rock slabs, jutting outward and layered one on top of another overtook the landscape. My grip tightened in his as he navigated us over the uneven knobby crevices. A rumbling and deafening roar vibrated in my eardrums, rocking against me and shaking the ground under my feet.

"Be careful, this next part's tricky. Hold on tight. It's single file through here."

One foot in front of the other, I matched each of his steps, left, right, left, right, getting more and more nervous as the slabs beneath our feet got narrower and narrower. "You know where you're goin' then?"

"Yeah, I come out here all the time."

Scared to look up or anywhere else but down, I asked with impatience, "Where are we?"

"Uh-uh, you'll see."

"Been there, done that," I mumbled.

"Don't be a grump."

"Stop driving me crazy," I yelled above the roar, adding a pinch to the back of his thigh and delivering my own form of retribution.

Without acknowledging me, he ventured onward. Either he didn't feel a thing or he played it off. "Believe me, you're going to love it."

"Yeah, yeah, that's what the slashers in horror movies say too." His enormous chuckles rolled over my chest, switching my mood from disgruntled to gooey in a flash.

Two gigantic rocks, one a beautiful burnished brown with moss covering most of it and the other reddish with striated black strips, provided minimal protection from the enormous gap on my left. A drop-off, of maybe twenty feet appeared endless from this height. If he hadn't been guiding the way, I would've turned around from fear. His careful but sure steps helped a teeny bit.

Less than a minute later, he came to a sudden stop, bumping my nose into his broad shoulder. As I took a step back, he tugged me forward and repositioned me, front and center.

A vista that needed to be experienced up close and personal appeared out of nowhere. The great beyond came to mind. When that day arrived, I wanted it to look like this.

Water—gushing over a jagged cliff into a dark green pool with cresting white caps. A raging stream below spouted and splashed upward with might.

Sunshine—beaming rays, darting at distinct points along the waterfall—revering the top, middle, and bottom.

Birds—swooping through the splashing and billowing waves. Melodies springing from their beaks in delight as they plunged head first into the water. As they ascended into flight with their catch, their squawking echoes resounded in the breeze, becoming cloaked in the willowy forest.

Linc wrapped his arms across my stomach, swaddling me tight. My temple resting against his cheek, I blessed the perfection and this precise point in time.

A stone ledge, several feet away, jutted out from underneath the waterfall. He escorted me beneath it, the spray baptizing our faces. Its sheer force commanding awe and filling me with tranquility.

"Worth the wait?"

"It's amazing." I placed my head on his chest and slid my freezing hands under his shirt, warming them against his heated skin.

"There's another spot close by." His fingers wove through mine, and he plotted a course downhill toward the gushing bank. Grassy reeds and cattails swayed as we swept past. Dragonflies whizzed back and forth along the rippling currents, lapping the pebbled shore. Chipmunks and birds chirped and scampered out of our way. Dried red leaves and clover curled beneath my steps. I glanced back. My footprints showed an imprint in a straight line, creating a map of the journey.

Not paying attention, I stumbled at a sudden change in the surface. Just as quick, he latched onto my elbows and kept me from falling.

"Wow." We ended up smack dab in the middle of a psychedelic array of wildflowers, surrounding us at every angle, a circular niche carved in the grass like a crop circle. "This is unreal."

A squeeze to my hand pulled my gaze away, and found Linc dropping to his knees at my feet. He brought my hands to his lips, kissing the top of one then the other. His silence didn't unnerve me much, but the way he kept biting his lips and the distress written all over his face amped my anxiety and concern. Not for me—for him.

I wiggled one of my hands out of his, and sifted it through his long hair, repeating the soothing motion. "What can I do to help you, Linc? Tell me and it's yours."

"Serena…" He dropped his forehead on my stomach, and his shuddering shoulders compelled me to hold him in a protective embrace like he'd done so often for me. My arms tightened until his breathing calmed and his shoulders relaxed.

He stood and pressed his temple to mine. Locked in his arms and hypnotic eyes, his sexy baritone whispered, "Make love to me."

Oh. My. God. I catapulted backward a foot or two, jolted by the unexpected request and the significance.

He frowned and examined every minute detail of my face. I had no idea if it showed anything, because all that registered was a thousand and one mini-explosions going off like fireworks inside of me, freezing me in place. If I dared to blink or move a muscle, I might miss the pivotal and momentous moment.

He reached his hand out to me and inched closer.

"No." My abrupt command stopped him mid-step and sent my feet forward, bringing me to where I first stood.

Long awaited anticipation drove me to shove his shirt over his head and toss it behind me. *Go ahead touch*, I heard my brain urge or maybe it had been him. Either way, I didn't allow my eyes or fingertips to miss out. Both christened his magnificent body by running up and down the curly hairs trailing the center of his abs, then right and left across his muscular pecs, blessing with devout and profound tender loving care.

So much better than observing from near or far.

"Take off my pants." His direct and to the point demand brought with it undeniable exhilaration.

Oh, yeah. My time had come—*finally.*

In ten seconds flat, I undid his belt and unzipped his jeans, sliding his boxers and pants down with expert proficiency. Again I found myself sitting at his feet, legs tucked behind me, bringing to mind a very embarrassing scene. That thought lasted less than it took to remove his clothes, because my eyes overruled my brain and eagerly explored his naked perfection, standing at ease in front of me.

He kicked off his shoes and dropped to his knees once more. "You want this? Want me?" His intense stare inspected mine for the slightest hint.

Was he out of his freaking mind?

Instead of answering, I planted a dainty kiss on his heart, the tiny hairs tickling my nose. Still as a statue, hands at his sides, he let me have free rein over the centerfold displayed just for me. His twitching muscles and labored breathing, a small indication my touch affected him as much as it did me, since my reaction was identical to his.

The new beginning and fresh start unveiled an adventurous side I'd kept hidden. Jumping jacks in my belly and a high like I'd never known kick-started my journey. I began at his nipple, licking all around it, and making sure I left my mark, nipping and sucking the tip between my teeth. His groans and clenching fists implied he liked it too.

An uncontrollable wicked smile joined my torturous investigation, which zigzagged from one side of his abs to the other, implanting each birthmark, sinking in every pore, and counting thousands of teensy hairs. That way, no matter near nor far, our bodies would always know and recognize the other, transcending space and time. I got as far as his belly button before he grabbed my shoulders and proceeded to remove my shirt, shorts, bra, and panties with such skilled efficiency it should've given me pause. But his desperate pursuit and undivided attention delighted me beyond belief.

Similar to Adam and Eve, naked as nature intended, a dreamlike and euphoric state embodied me as he held me in his arms, one of them wrapped around my lower back, the other pressed between my breasts, his hand cupping my cheek. Exposed in broad daylight, his customary misty eyes transformed to a dazzling and transparent blue, fusing with my sea-green ones and blending into a serene turquoise mirrored in our combined gaze—peace replacing intensity.

Caught up in his blissful expression, I hardly noticed the breeze blowing hair in our faces. It wasn't until he leaned forward and grazed an endearing kiss on my temple, on my cheeks, and on my lips that all my senses kicked in. Attuned and in-sync with him, I repeated the same actions. After I did, he whispered in my ear, "Many are the stars I see but in my eye no star like thee."

My eyes closed, capturing the sentiment in my heart and soul. The roaring waterfall and endless twittering animals stilled, as if nature and all its glory recognized our unique union and wanted to cherish it too.

He pulled me on top of him, lying in the grass, wildflowers surrounding us and swaying in tune to our heartbeats. Heat from the sunshine surged through my veins, dotting sweat on my brow and trickling down my spine. Boyish exuberance stretched across his lips, a blush brushed his cheeks, and his expression, one of awe, mimicked my emotions and increased my awareness of what would happen next.

Before I could get more comfortable, he rolled me beneath him, and sprang up on his knees.

"What are you—"

He pressed his fingers on my mouth, riffled through the pockets of his pants with his other hand, and held up a condom. A dimpled, devilish grin appeared as he lifted my arm and dropped the crinkling wrapper in my palm.

"What am I supposed to do with that?" Yep, my idiotic babbling struck again. Ugh!

He chuckled and tore it open, pinching it between my fingers.

"I'm all yours." He scooted forward, bringing his bobbing cock a nose length away.

Oh, sweet heaven.

My eyes crossed while I stared at the enlarged head, clear fluid dotting the slit.

Holy smokes.

Swirling my pinky through the indent, I spread the cream around the ridged head, careful to gloss the mound using methodical precision. His heaving chest and measured breaths coordinated in a rapid beat with mine as I grasped his length and pumped it up and down.

Since I'd never tasted a man before, I was willing to give it a concentrated beginner's effort, but a bout of shyness hit me. Unwilling to let this opportunity be missed, I swiped my finger over the dripping liquid and sucked it between my parted lips. A salty taste embodied with his distinctive scent infused my blood with a craving addiction. Delicious.

"You're driving me fucking nuts." He positioned the object still clasped in my hand to the spot I'd just been. "Condom on, now."

Ha! Mr. Bossy Pants getting impatient. Served him right for torturing me for months, leaving me frustrated and horny.

Zeroed in and focused, my shaky hands unrolled it, covering him from tip to base. Now I was the one wearing the wicked smile extended ear to ear like a little girl who'd been waiting all year to ride her first loopty-loop, super-speedy coaster, discovering she superseded the restrictions.

Yeah for me!

"Beautiful," he whispered, cupping my breasts and brushing a thumb over each pointed nipple. He leaned down and inhaled, coddling them against his cheek and then flicking his tongue once…twice…three times on each. I arched up, using his muscled biceps as my anchor. My moans alerting Mother Nature and every other creature in a five-mile radius to our carnal acts.

His slid his hand between my legs, pressing his thumb on the nub. My hips pumped up and down, repeating the same as my wordless mouth—more, no less—more, less—definitely *more*. Then out loud. "Please."

"What do you want? Tell me." He gazed into my eyes and waited for my response.

Caught up in the emotions, it took me a while to form coherent words. "Give me you. *All* of you."

"Tell me again," he whispered, clasping our hands together and placing them above my head, and in the same breath he slid his shaft halfway inside me.

Somehow I knew what he wanted and needed. In response, I set my mouth to his temple and professed, "I love you."

At his lips, I murmured, "I love you."

Melded to his heart, I pledged, "I love you" at the same time, I lunged my hips up with all my might, driving him home—right where he belonged.

Chapter Twenty-One

Mylaynee's witty and comical attitude had me busting a gut half the time. Add Fallon, Paulette, and Sage to the mix and we didn't have a dry eye in the Fab Five group. Being with them had fulfilled my life in ways I never could've anticipated.

After everything that happened yesterday I needed some girl time. Instead of jumping head first into invoicing facts and figures, I rounded up the crew at first light. Relaxing in lounge chairs, one beside the other like an assembly line, the yelling out and trash-talking resembled a rowdy classroom.

"I have news." My announcement delivered at megaphone level, while I teetered on the edge of my seat, a fist pressed to my upper lip, barely able to contain the giddiness bubbling inside.

Silence. Geez, they never shut it that fast before.

"Uh, okay, this one's for our jinx-vault—not a word or you'll be cursed for life." We extended our knuckles to each other for a fist bump, and at the same time I made them promise not to tell anyone. In unison they agreed, completing the ritual.

"I told Linc I love him."

Each registered different expressions. Mylaynee: breaking open the piggy bank smile. Fallon and Paulette: clapping hands and high fives. Sage: a scrunched nose and tongue stuck out, wiggling her eyebrows up and down, including a lascivious motion with her fingers and thumb.

When they settled down, Paulette revealed, "We knew that a long time ago. Took you how long to say it?" She glanced down at her arm and imaginary watch and then fake smacked me in the head.

As they giggled at my expense, I plunked back in my seat and crossed my arms. "Fine! See if I tell you guys anything anymore."

They roared even louder.

Mylaynee broke through the revelry claiming, "Just remember—*I* was the one that introduced you."

Damn, I loved that girl. Crushing bear hugs all around, the uproar that followed resembled an assembly full of teenage girls' catcalls and indecent ribbing about the hottest boy in school.

Riding the high, I gave myself a mental pat on the back. That wasn't as hard as I thought it would be.

Until Sage said, "Did he tell you too?"

Chills rocketed up my spine, giving me an instant brain freeze. Entangled in all the discoveries and emotions yesterday, it didn't compute until now.

"Serena…" Mylaynee called my name, but it sounded far off, even though she sat right next to me. A buzzing in my ears drowned her out and bile rose in my throat. My rapid swallowing didn't help keep it down very well. "Are you all right, honey? You look pale. Do you need to lie down?"

She clasped the side of my face, inspecting my eyes. "Sage, go get her some water." Her hands moved from my cheeks to my shoulders and down to my ice-cold hands. She kneeled in front of me and held them tight. "Talk to me, sweetie."

A water glass appeared in my view. Sage placed it to my lips. "Open up. Drink." She insisted like a mother trying to force medicine down her child's throat.

Breathe.

Inhale deep. Exhale slow.

Repeat.

That helped get my stomach somewhat under control. I shook the fuzz from my head and grabbed the glass, drinking it to the bottom and plunking it down on the table. "Sorry, I'm not sure, I'm, uh…not feeling well."

They looked at each other. Sage, Paulette, and Fallon left. Mylaynee remained crouched at my knees. After a few seconds of studying my face, she nodded and yanked me up from the seat and tucked me into bed.

Without another word, she left me alone.

Exactly what I needed.

"Serena? Wake up."

As my dream of a knight in shining armor galloping away from a crying fair maiden disappeared into the fog, a deep and worried voice pulled me from the mist.

"Are you okay?" A gentle hand brushed through my hair and a solid heat pressed along my back, waking me. I turned my groggy head and came head on with Linc. Worry lines creased his forehead and around his mouth. My stomach clenched at the unknown concern and my brain began to register my surroundings. The sound—boats honking; the smell—woodsy-citrus; the sight—gorgeous and distressed.

"Linc," I croaked, clearing my throat, "what's wrong?" I cupped his chin and brushed my thumb along his frown.

He removed a few strands of hair from my eyes and tucked them behind my ear, surveying my prone body. "You sick?"

"No, why?" The clock indicated it was noon. "What are you doing here?"

"I came to…I have something…we need to talk."

My chest tightened as early morning memories clamored in my head. My legs tingled not from falling asleep or lack of blood flow but numbness from his ominous and halting message. I stayed silent. Thoughts casting me back to my fading dream. Did telling him I loved him freak him out?

"It's important."

I sat up and leaned against the headboard, waiting to find out my fate.

He sucked in a deep breath, diverted his gaze to the windows, and said to himself, "Okay…" After what seemed like forever, he locked his sight on me and foretold my future. "I want to make some changes around here, with you."

Oh, God he's gonna get rid of me. Fire me. Kick me out.

A new medical term needed to be classified for a heart's death-defying leap, head first into a bottomless pit in my stomach. I'd be a prime candidate for the case study. Bile once again rose in my mouth, almost gagging me.

Straight-faced and with a serious business demeanor, he declared, "I've been thinking about a lot of things, but I need…want you to hear me out first, without interrupting."

I hadn't said much yet. How could I? This had bad news written all over it. All I could manage was a dip of my chin, so I wouldn't expel the entire contents rolling in my belly.

"I own several night clubs, not like this one. I've been handling the books, but I don't like it. I could've hired someone before, but I like control." A sly smirk pitch-hit in the corner of his mouth, and the dimple, hidden most of the time came out full force, along with his blushing cheeks. His deadpan expression switched to puppy face adorable in an instant.

"I thought, maybe…I could hire you." He shrugged his shoulders and pulled my hand into his. "If you want, I'd like you to schedule the appointments too." My mouth dropped open, and he rushed through the rest. "I'd pay you. I think it'd be good for everyone. You wouldn't have to bartend or go to the lounge, if you don't want to."

He bent down, kissed the top of my hand, and when he glanced up his shoulders relaxed and twenty years seemed to vanish, lightening his features. "What do you say?"

"Why?" I blurted, since it was all I could get my brain and mouth to put together.

He whispered, "You really don't know?"

I shook my head, returning to my mute state.

"Hmm…" He slid me onto his lap and set my head on his comforting shoulder. "Do you remember when I told you someday you'd have what you wanted?" I nodded. How could I forget? Until recently, it replayed in my mind on permanent rewind. "My someday came yesterday, Serena. A gift and honor you gave—to *me*." My arms squeezed his ribs hard, and I looked up, needing to see his face. He smiled and pecked me on the nose. "Many are the stars I see but in my eye no star like thee." His sincere gaze and deep baritone recited the verse like a ballad composed and sung just for me. "Did you hear me say it before?"

"Yes," I whispered, brushing my fingers across his lips.

His smile increased a hundredfold. "So you do listen to me?" For that smart-ass comment, I stuck my tongue out at him. He chased after it, sucking it into his mouth.

Our bodies repositioned, me underneath him, his hair draped both sides of my face, creating our own private haven. "When you came in for the interview…" He paused and shifted his hand through my hair, twirling the strands around his fingers. "Destiny granted me a wish…one I've never spoken out loud. *Ever.* If I did, temptation would somehow alter fate's hand."

He set his temple on mine and continued to melt my heart. "There's a poem that reminds me of you, and when we met." I didn't even know what it would be yet, and my eyes moistened, realizing the rarity of such revelations from this private and reserved man. "It goes like this… once, not long ago, a shooting star so brilliant and magnificent appeared in the daylight. The rare and once in a lifetime vision ignited my heart and captured my soul…a wish fulfilled, when your light transformed me at first sight."

Too overwhelmed to respond, I chose a more universal expression—making love to a tune created from two different styles, yet harmonized as one.

The melody—this man—inscribed on my heart for all eternity.

I reversed the tables. "We need to talk." The echoing words sounded so menacing, but this time maybe they were. He grasped my chin and tilted it so I had no choice but to look up at him. As much as I wanted to avoid his eyes, I didn't. I needed to put my big girl pants on and ask once and for all. "Where does this leave me? I mean, I'll accept your offer. But what about the other thing?" Okay, maybe I still wore training pants.

"What *thing*?"

I buried my head in his neck and mumbled, "Being exclusive. What does that mean?"

His lengthy silence made insecurities I thought buried reappear. "You dumping me, Serena?"

I shot straight up and stared him down. "No," my voice squawked like a parrot.

"I don't know, sounds like you don't want to be my girl."

If he didn't have a big-ass grin on his face, I would've thought he was serious. "Did you *ask* me to be your girl? 'Cause I don't remember hearing that." I tossed him the same expression, upping it with a "What you gonna do about it?" sassy attitude. Take that, smarty pants.

He threw the covers back, pulled on a pair of shorts and dashed out of the room.

What the hell?

Faster than a sixty-second commercial and with both hands behind his back, he plunked down on the bed, bouncing me into his shoulder. His lips a centimeter from mine, but not kissing them, he deposited something in my hand and fisted it closed.

If I wanted to find out what it was, I needed to sit back and look.

Inside my palm, a hand-cut, pink heart made from the decorative notepad I had next to my computer. Written in his handwriting it said…

Serena,

Will you be my girl?

Yes or No.

My hand fixed on his heart, I used an index finger to spell my answer.

Chapter Twenty-Two

Thanks to the ridiculous amount of money Linc agreed to pay me, I'd be able to save a chunk and make substantial payments in the process. His savvy investments in several cities showed a lucrative bottom line. No matter what he said, his record keeping had been impeccable. I expected nothing less. Control freak or not, it wasn't his style to do anything halfway.

Luck had finally taken a turn in my favor, and I attributed it to Gram's spirit duking it out for her granddaughter, a vision that had me laughing. *You go, Gram. Show'em who's boss.*

Appointment manager came with a lot more responsibility than I ever thought. My first day began with a crash course in encryption and record-keeping procedures. Linc provided a secure tablet PC and asked that it be kept in his office safe when not used. Without question I agreed. No way I'd want to be the cause of sensitive information falling into the wrong hands. The rest of the week involved the scheduling process for on- and off-site appointments, security arrangements, and gathering information about employee preferences.

He wanted anyone attending an outside event to have a "chaperone," his term for it. My term: bodyguard. His hypervigilance ignored the fact that each client went through a vetting process better than one completed by the FBI. Security personnel had to be in place, regardless, no arguments. Since Sal coordinated that part, I spent quite a bit of time learning the ins and outs. After the multi-session trainings my head spun from the enormity and the pressure, making sure to dot every *i* and cross each *t*. How the heck had Linc done this for so long without help?

Determined not to let him down, I sought guidance from a trusted source. I entered Mylaynee's apartment after knocking twice and came to a whiplash stop.

"Uh sorry, I didn't mean to interrupt."

"I was just leaving." Jax strolled toward me carrying a thick folder. "Later, Serena," he said to my back, using a professional rather than sex-laced voice and avoiding eye contact as he exited.

"Come sit down, girl." Mylaynee patted the cushion that he'd left and tucked her legs up.

I pointed a thumb to the vacant door and complained, "I still can't believe you're friends with that jackass."

She shook her head like a fawning mother does when a child does something naughty, but looks so darn cute doing it. "Aw, but he's such a McDreamy."

"Oh, he's a babe magnet alright and loves stickin' it to anybody."

Her head tilted back, and it took her a minute to calm her howling laughter and clear her watering eyes. "Girl, how many times do I have to tell you he gets off on rilin' you. That's how he is."

"Doesn't matter, I'd love give him a knock-out punch right to his big-ass mouth. Freakin' jerk."

She shook her head and wagged her finger at me like I'd done something wrong. "He's not so bad. Men like him can't help struttin' their feathers. Deep, *deep* down though, he's a good guy, and not a bad one to have on your side."

"Whatever, I'll do without, thank you very much. So what's he want now? You working for him again?"

"Yeah, there's a case he needs help with." She picked up a folder from the table, similar to the one Jax had, and flipped through a few pages. "You should give it a try. He pays top dollar."

"Seriously? You're kidding, right? I can't stand being in the same room with him, let alone listen to more of his crap. No way. I don't care how desperate I get."

"It's *fun*," she emphasized the word, needling me with her elbow. "Change of pace, you know? His company does all kinds a stuff. It's cool and I love it," she professed with a wistful, dreamy look. "You might not see me for the next few days. If it takes longer I'll let you know, okay?"

I nodded, my mind drifting to the trust fund playboy, astonished he was capable of running a multimillion-dollar business. Ranked at the top in the industry, his company had a stellar reputation and happened to include the best-trained professionals around. Go figure.

Mylaynee's interest in "other" work reminded me of the reason I came here in the first place. Jax shoved aside, I pressed on to more important matters. "I need your advice about the appointments."

"Uh, yeah girl, the word is out. Warning, the hornets are swarming. Watch your back, if you know what I mean."

I knew exactly what—*who* she meant.

Sex Education 101. Meeting with everyone took quite a bit of time, but the conversations increased my vocabulary a hundredfold, enough to create my own explicit dictionary. The intimate details catalogued in the tablet PC, including likes and dislikes, on- or off-site, work hours, schedule preferences, and on and on. It boggled my mind that Linc had it all memorized. Since I wouldn't be able to do that and wanted to connect on a personal level, my plan of attack, and one Mylaynee agreed would work well, involved meeting with each employee. After each visit, the mental images and documentation expanded my knowledge base, and described in full detail sexual practices, fetishes, BDSM, and a bunch of other terms never mentioned in the erotica novels I read. Thank goodness for Google. I created a glossary that had at least ten pages, explaining any term I didn't understand, or was too embarrassed to ask about. Goodness, I never realized sex could be so complex.

I stood outside the last apartment, my stomach twisting in knots. After I knocked, the door flew open, showcasing a five-foot-four pain in the ass in nothing more than a see-through pink teddy.

"What do you want, Sadrena?"

Okay, Gram wherever you are, beam it down, woman, because I need the almighty powers for this one. "You have some time to talk?"

She leaned against the door frame, her face contorted and shriveled up like a prune. "You think you won?"

Gram, now would be great.

Ignoring her, I pressed on. "If you and Tanya have a few minutes, I'd like to discuss the appointments."

"I do it *all, Sad*rena, in bed and out. Maybe you should be the one making an appointment with *me,* so I can school *you.* Oh, wait a minute…" She stood straight and clipped the tablet in my hand, causing me to readjust my grip so it didn't drop. "We don't have nursery school around here, so you'll have to go somewhere far, far away." She propped her hand on her hip, long manicured daggers at the ready—to claw my eyes out.

"I'm not going anywhere. You don't have to like me, but I have a job to do, and it'd be better if you worked *with* me. If not, then you'll have to take whatever you get."

Thanks, Gram.

"I *get* plenty and *give* just as good. Ask Linc. He told me about your pathetic attempts to seduce him. We laughed about it in *my* bed. Maybe that would be great conversation for *your* appointment, Sadrena. With me."

Shit. Shit. Shit. She needed a snake named after her, because that hiss—toxic. Her sting paralyzed me, my vision turning pitch black. Woozy, I slapped air before clutching the wall. My confidence disintegrated as an image of the two of them in bed wouldn't stop replaying in my head.

Her cackling ricocheted through the hall, causing my head to spin all over again. No doubt my continued silence disclosed the internal damage, all the air and fortitude knocked right out of me. Damn it. Anytime she mentioned Linc it made me sick, even now, after all that had happened between *us*. I still hadn't asked him about her yet, my old insecurities and fear of losing another vital person in my life overtook my actions. A risk I wasn't willing to take this early in our relationship. The fire in my stomach told me otherwise, since all I wanted to do was bitch-slap her straight to hell. But after the poison she spewed, my jaw locked in place, keeping me from forming a coherent sound.

"Serena, can I see you a minute?"

Behind me appeared a guardian angel and my saving grace, Mylaynee. The stink eye she directed at B.B. promised her own brand of retribution. I drew in a long inhale and then exhaled real slow, settling my nerves a bit. Temporary reinforcements like Mylaynee helped too. Her grinding knuckles in my lower back and clearing throat renewed my focus on the job at hand. When I turned around, a door slammed in my face. Her final answer, I guess.

Great, just freaking great.

"How was your day?" Linc crouched down and inspected my face better than a police officer on DUI patrol. Mannequin mask in place, I chopped and diced with Master Chef proficiency. Performing under his intense scrutiny, however, caused me to sweat bullets. "Dinner will be ready soon. Grilled steak and veggies okay?"

He tugged the knife out of my hand and pointed toward the couch. "Go put your feet up. Read one of your *steamy* books." His lovey-dovey high-schoolish taunt dared, but also promised an erotic pay-off. "I'll take care of everything." He shoved me gently in the right direction, and for once I didn't argue and ran out to the balcony, hopping onto one of the lounge chairs. My unpleasant thoughts vanished, replaced with sex, sex, and more sex. I loved reading—and *him*.

A dose of fresh air, sunshine, and one of my favorite erotic books transformed my attitude to naughty in the time it took to read one page. My mental list included a dozen X-rated acts I wanted to perform on Linc. This story had a hot private detective who used his handcuffs in very wanton ways. As I read, the story progressed to the cold case he had been working on. An earlier conversation came to mind, spurring me to do a little probing of my own when Linc came outside to put food on the grill. "How long have you known Jax?"

My out-of-the-blue question had him whipping around with a scowl on his face. Instead of answering, he concentrated on making perfect criss-cross marks. "Since diapers." His response not coming until after I'd read another page.

I nodded even though he couldn't see me. "Did you go to school together?"

"Yeah." He responded with a shrug. "His dad went to college with mine. They were frat brothers and best friends.

After my parents died, and what I'd gone through with Belinda, Jax got me back on my feet. He loaned me some money for her care and got me started in the nightclub business. His parents went to bat with the judge, said they'd watch out for us. It convinced him to grant custody. I've repaid Jax every penny, but I owe his family much more than that. I couldn't have survived without them."

Huh, maybe he wasn't such a bad guy after all. Two people close to him sang his praises. I don't know, perhaps it took a while to get to know him, revealing the real prize underneath. Hmm, I guess time would tell.

My rapid curiosity urged me on, and I couldn't resist from venturing into taboo territory. "He's an attractive guy—" Linc stiffened, shutting me up in an instant. Yeah, that hadn't come out the way I'd wanted. Besides, it hadn't been what I'd meant. Even so I didn't need to call attention to him in quite that way. Sex-on-a-stick, beyond Donald Trump rich, Jax baffled me.

Should I listen to the prickles along my neck telling me to shut the heck up?

"Why does he…use the services?" The best wording I could come up with, omitting the "every night" at least. Once again, my determined brain continued to ignore common sense.

On a very loud exhale, his laser beam gaze narrowed with pinpoint precision—on me. "Why you asking?"

"Just curious."

He slammed the metal spatula down and shot forward, aiming for his target and marching toward my chair.

"I…" Stunned by his reaction I stuttered, "I-I'll drop it." I flicked to the next page and tried to ignore his fired-up presence, which overtook half my seat, his heated thigh pressed against mine. He removed the book from my hands and set it on my lap, dog-earing the page.

"Let's not talk about him, okay?"

I flipped open the novel and fake scanned the words, playing off the entire exchange. "No biggie, forget I said anything." The disappointment in my voice came out even though I tried to contain it. I'd thought we'd made much more progress than that, and I could finally *talk* to him.

My book fell out of my hands and onto the cement when he tossed me over his shoulder. Silent, determined Linc had a new target—the bedroom.

Discussion over.

Dinner forgotten and burned to a crisp.

Chapter Twenty-Three

My hands full of overflowing grocery bags, I exited the elevator and entered a busier than usual hallway. Tanya and B.B. huddled together, Sal next to them, each directing their attention on me. Sal glanced at his watch and back up, casting an *I've been looking all over for you* squinty-eyed glare. "I need to talk to you. It's important."

B.B. whispered in Tanya's ear. Their uncontained snickers perturbed and scared me at the same time. Lined up on either side of Sal like mega-watt speakers, their open mouths and scrutinizing gaze flitting between Sal and me, preparing to blast to the world, "Off with her head." Behind Sal's back, B.B. sliced a finger across her throat and then pointed it at me, waving ba-bye and lipping the warning.

Crap, now what?

Sal took the bags from me and waited as I unlocked the door. "Thanks." I entered the kitchen and flicked my hand toward the counter. "Set them there. Do you mind? I'd like to get the cold stuff in the fridge."

"Need help?"

"Nope, I got it." I motioned him toward the living room and got everything put away in record time. Seated across from one another, my stomach twisted in a thousand knots while I waited for an explanation. Unsure whether it had to do with work or something else, either way, I had an eerie feeling.

In slow motion, he stuck a hand in his suit jacket and tossed a photo on the coffee table. "You know her?"

I jumped up on wobbly legs and clutched my knees, a full-blown panic attack blasting me to smithereens. Sal lunged around the table and grabbed my shoulders. "Sit down. You're going to pass out."

Buzzing in my ears drowned him out, my arrhythmic breathing and head-to-toe tremors locked me in a bent over position. His strong hands grasped my armpits. The unspoken support caused my legs to buckle, dropping me into the chair. He grabbed my neck and shoved it down, my head lodged between my knees. "Take slow, deep breaths. In…out…in…out. Follow mine…that's it. Yeah, in, out, in, out, Serena." He crouched down, his concerned gaze measuring mine. "You're doing it. Take your time."

Sometime later, I composed myself. When I did, sweat dripped down the sides of my face and my T-shirt clung to me like a straitjacket. To counteract the effects, I gulped down a couple bottles of water, attempting to rejuvenate my dehydrated and shocked system. On the edge of my seat, I picked up the picture in my shaky hands and stared at my greatest heartache and embarrassment.

"I take it you know her then."

"No…yes…no," I whispered, hesitating, then faced him head on, revealing the truth. "She's my mother."

"Shit." He stood, rubbing a hand down his face. "Are you trying to stop her? Did you tell anybody?"

I stood and paced the room, yanking on my hair, and most likely pulling it out at the roots. "Not yet." My scared-to-death clipped answer came out followed by a sigh.

He stepped in front of me, bringing me to a stutter-stop. "What can I do to help?"

My jaw clenched tight, I glanced at the photo. "You tell anyone?"

"If you mean Linc? No. You need to tell him."

Ignoring the directive, I opened the sliding glass doors and took a breath of fresh air. A gusty wind and torrential rain drenched the patio, the choppy waves twisting and turning, and churning along with my nerves. I massaged my temple and tried to figure out how to address this unexpected turn of events. "I need some time. Can you give me that?"

"Serena—"

My raised hand cut him off. "I need to hire an attorney or private eye or something."

He walked over to me and set his hand on my shoulder. "Let me have Jax help."

"Uh uh, no way, Sal, please, don't tell him, promise me," I rushed out, crushing his arm in a vise grip in the process.

"Calm down, don't be getting yourself worked up again."

"It's my problem, I'll take care of it. How'd you find out?"

"Come on, I taught you security procedures this week. Did you forget about the background checks?"

"But you ran mine before. You didn't say anything, why now?"

He shook his head and explained the process again. "There's different levels, remember? I ran a deeper check when you took over the accounts. The transactions on your statements didn't make sense. They were from all over the US before and after the time you were living here. I knew it couldn't be you making that many. You're frugal to a fault." He chuckled when I shot him a pointed look, shrugging it off he continued. "It bothered me, gnawed at my investigative instincts, so I kept digging."

Damn. I dropped into the chair and covered my face with my hands, massaging my brows in a circular motion. The extra weight from this screwed up situation and my elbows drilling into my thighs multiplied the pain in my head and jolted a nerve pinching fire through the rest of me.

Oh, Gram. If she'd known her daughter stole my identity it would've broken her heart. It sure did mine. My so-called mother used my social security number to open credit cards and take out loans to the tune of fifty grand. It didn't end there. She kept using my name, taking whatever she could. Her greed far-reaching. The ultimate cost—my childhood home.

I'd discovered her deceit a few months before Gram's death, when I got denied for a loan. I should've hired an attorney right away, but with everything going on I didn't. And in a way, a part of me was in denial too. The fact that my own flesh and blood could do such a thing not only disgusted me, it stabbed me in the heart all over again. After the initial shock wore off, I buried myself in work and took care of Gram.

Now though, I had no excuse. Sal finding out had been a good thing. It forced me to wake the heck up, and take steps to crawl out of the hole and despair she put me in. I pulled Sal into a hug, squeezing him so hard he blushed and tugged at his shirt collar. "Now don't be gettin' fresh. If you're trying to get out of telling Linc, think again." A strong Boston accent I hadn't heard from him before came out of nowhere.

"Figured me out, huh?"

"He's going to want to help, Serena."

I directed my gaze outdoors and muttered, "It's not fair to him. He has enough to worry about."

"If he finds out I kept this from him—"

"Don't worry about it. Let me be the one to tell him, okay?"

He nodded, and on the way out shouted a last-ditch offer. "Let me know if there's anything I can do."

Chapter Twenty-Four

Clearer weather enticed me outdoors, providing a much-needed temporary escape. I walked along the boardwalk and watched tadpoles and baby bluegills eat the insects on top. Poor, helpless bugs going about their day not realizing in mere seconds they'd be swallowed up in one fell swoop.

Yep, knew how that felt.

Mylaynee's uncanny ability to fit matters into an appropriate perspective would help right about now. But she wasn't home yet. Still working on a case, I saw her just a few minutes here and there this week. Our brief exchanges hadn't provided many details about the job, so I had no idea what Jax had gotten her involved in. Regardless, she enjoyed the work and her happiness mattered most. I'd just ignore the fact he had any part in it or contributed to her excitement. He didn't deserve the credit, she did. A genuine beauty inside and out, I was blessed to have her as a friend. Her unconditional love and support knew no bounds. She always had my back, and I'd do anything for her.

I flicked a rock onto the water; it hopped once, twice, three times before sinking. Not bad. About to try again, my cell rang. Not recognizing the number I answered hesitantly. When the voice called out my name in one short clip, requesting a meeting in his office *now*, the stone in my hand fell, stabbing my pinky toe. Dang it. I told Sal I'd handle it.

The entire way to his office I picked through a thousand and one reasons for not telling him. Maybe throwing myself at his mercy would work. Secrets weren't a good way to start a relationship. That much I did know, even with my limited experience.

Linc and Sal huddled around the desk, a map spread across the top. Jax on the phone, yelling at someone about FUBAR, whatever that meant.

"Is something wrong?" Like a victim about to testify on the stand, I reserved the big reveal for the pivotal moment. At this time, I'd take a "don't give away too much information" stance. All responses would be abridged and concise. Especially with probable hostile spectators in the room. I glanced between Linc and Sal, trying to gauge the already charged atmosphere. Jax pacing around the room, rustling his spiky hair similar to the yanking I'd done earlier, didn't help reassure me any.

"Yeah, *we* have a problem."

I bit my lip and shot a glare in Sal's direction. Fingers pressed to my temple, I rubbed, stirring the jumbled thoughts and making it hard to articulate. "Uh, I, um, you see, I…" My hand dropped to my throat. I pinched it between my thumb and forefinger several times, forcing something coherent to come up to my tongue.

Before it did, Linc ushered me into the lounge, closing the door behind him. "I need you to do something for me." The worry lines on his temple were back, and I felt awful for putting them there.

Ready to spill my guts, I spouted, "Anything." Okay, maybe not. Apparently my cotton mouth decided to filter any testimony first to determine if it would be defensible.

"I don't want you to worry. I'll take care of everything."

"Linc, n—"

Not letting me finish, he grabbed my shoulders and held me still. Then the worst possible doomsday prophecy happened. One I never could have predicted. "It's Mylaynee, Serena. The job she was doing went wrong. We're going to get her."

Oh, dear God. No.

The pulse pounding in my neck and heartbeat thumping in my ears were precursors to the red-hot fury burning in my belly. "Where is that jackass? I'm gonna kill him. Jax!" I shoved his hands off me and made a mad dash for the office. Two sure-fire arms grabbed me around the waist and lifted me off my feet, flip-flops dangling from my toes.

"Settle down." He urged without putting me back down.

I twisted around a teensy-bit, as far as I could move in his locked embrace. My eyeballing didn't do much to intimidate, but I clenched his arms and pushed, putting me nose to nose and hopefully communicating the threat loud and clear. "You tell that SOB if anything happens to her. He. Will. Pay."

"We're loaded up. Gotta go," Sal called out from the doorway and disappeared in a blur.

Linc set me back on my feet, took hold of my face and promised, "I'll call you as soon as I have her."

"Can I go?"

"No."

"But—"

"I need you here. We have a full house and without Sal and me around you're it. Will you do that?"

"Okay," I said halfheartedly. "She's not hurt, is she? You'd tell me, right?"

He cupped my cheek, and I leaned in to it, holding my breath. "I don't know."

I wrapped my arms around his chest, giving him a bear hug so gigantic it could stretch around Mylaynee no matter how far away. "*Please* bring her home, and be careful."

When he vamoosed, I booked it the heck out of there too—warp speed.

Special request, Gram. Please watch over them.

My car idling outside the apartment building, it didn't take long before I sighted my target—Linc's SUV. As I coasted along some distance apart, I glanced at the dash. Two hours until the lounge opened. Just in case, I called Fallon on my way out and told her to hold down the fort. Linc would never know.

He drove to the West Side and turned onto Pier Street, swerving into an alley. Crap. Abandoned years ago, this section had one decrepit building after another lining the dock.

All three of them exited, taking off at a swift jog. Not far behind, I hoofed it too, praying they didn't see me. At the next street, they turned out of view. That was when I picked up speed, sprinting faster than I ever had, rounding the corner in enough time to see them split apart and head in three different directions. Sal went left and Linc right, disappearing between two buildings.

Making a quick decision, I followed Jax. His case, his business, I figured he'd take the lead. Too many turns and blocks later, I lost count and had no clue how to get back. At the end of the street, Jax opened a door and entered a dilapidated warehouse that could be used for a horror movie. Double crap.

I got closer and ducked into a nook that might have been an exit at one time, but the graffiti-tagged particleboard and criss-crossed two-by-fours closed it off. The dimming daylight and eerie silence gave me the creeps. Okay, maybe this wasn't such a bright idea.

Time stood still the longer I remained in the squished space. How in the heck did police put up with stakeouts? Whatever time I'd been here drove me bat-shit crazy. Antsy and determined to find out something, I crept away from my hiding spot. As I skulked around the corner, I rammed head first into a brick wall, my body bouncing backward and then yanked forward, coming face to scar-face with a man wider than a linebacker. "Lookin' fa' som'on' missy?" A jagged slash marked the entire bridge of his nose, slitting the left nostril in half. Hash marks scored his cheek, its gashes etching slots down to his jaw and extending to his earlobe.

Note to self: *do not follow Jax. Ever.*

He spun me around so fast I fell forward onto my hands and knees. Before I could dash away, he wrapped his arms around my waist and slammed a solid object into my lower back, surging an excruciating pain up my spine. I snapped my head back, ramming it into his chin. Sewer breath hit my nose as he growled, "Move, that'a way." The gun jabbing into my kidney registered, classifying my idiocy as mistake #2: blondes *didn't* do it better…they made you stupid. He clamped onto my upper arm with a fist of steel and hip checked me forward. Stuck together like glue, we shuffled in unison one foot after another, his steel-toe boots scraping my Achilles tendon. On my next step, the idiot's knee butted into mine, buckling it. I stumbled, twisting my ankle. He wrenched my elbow and snapped me back into his chest, jamming the weapon into my ribs and launching a raging ache unlike any other I'd experienced before. Doubled over, I clutched my arms around my stomach, sucking in much-needed oxygen.

Jax crashed through a door at the opposite end, forcing my head to pop up from my hunched over position.

"Rick, let her go."

"No can do, J."

"Come on man, she's no problem. Serena, come here," he called out with exasperation, waving his hand and slapping it against his side like the puppy he'd been training hadn't listened to his command.

My height and combined muscle from jogging every day had its advantages at times. But no matter how hard I twisted and jerked the outcome remained the same, a pitiful result even though I used my full body weight. The goon attached to me like a monkey on my back had his own solid mass, outweighing me by at least a hundred pounds and anchoring me to the spot.

Alright, Serena, think.

In a blink, Sal and Linc appeared, apparitions materializing in the distance, but too remote to cast a spell on the evildoer who held me in captivity.

"Serena," Linc yelled, taking off in a full-out run and charging toward me. A slower and shorter Sal trailed behind him.

The stabbing pressure on my back released, and in that instant my view shifted from a crazed Linc to the gun next to my ear, pointing right at him.

My brain, overwrought from the intense situation and exorbitant amounts of stress, splintered from rational thought, and in a split second I threw myself on Rick. Momentum, gravity, and forces unknown took hold, both of us caught in an unfortunate game of chicken. My side—unbalanced and steering empty-handed. Rick's—laying on the gun power.

Fire ignited. The impact so jarring the implosion crumpled me to the ground, smacking my forehead into the cracked and crumbled cement. Hands and arms spread out, scraping flesh, I cushioned some of the blow.

Rick gone. Jax rolled me over, tore off his shirt, and pushed it down on my right side, knocking my gasping breaths out of me. Linc hauled me into his arms and dashed off at break-neck speed. His furtive glances and quick examinations assessed the damage while he hightailed it out of there. Sweat poured off him as he darted down one street and another. My aching head slipped off his shoulder, propelling my immobile weight backward and suspending my neck at an awkward angle that swayed with each stomp.

Linc propped open the back hatch and my body slid off his knee, rocking me from my stupor. He crawled inside, carrying me in his arms. My head cradled in his lap, he tossed his sweat-stained shirt off too. The force he used and the immense pressure building inside me drove my shallow breaths out in a gush again. His blurry eyes scrutinized and inspected every scrape, each bruise, and the bloody, gaping hole.

Jax and Sal hopped in the front of the SUV and sped us away. Linc barking orders, while Jax and Sal shouted, "How's she doing?" "How bad?"

Transcendent effects happened not right away, but gradually. Body and mind separated, taking independent journeys, undisclosed and concealed from the other. Hazy blue eyes faded out, then in, and out again.

Memories flickered like a silent movie Kinetoscope, one flashback to the next.

The first encounter: the office—meeting Linc—a new job. Fate's bearing encouraging, "Yes, this is the way."

The sailboat: a changing tide—sharing beliefs, exposing a little bit about ourselves—destiny bringing two searching souls together.

The unsurpassable consummation: making love surrounded by nature—an unforeseen union—dream made reality.

Linc's soft but insistent lips kissed…
my temple,

my eyelids,
my cheeks,
my lips.
Cleansing each with heart-wrenching tears.
Don't cry, Linc.
Everything will be...

Chapter Twenty-Five

In a sterile room, slumped in a hard-back chair, a defeated man sat frozen in an endless, tortured stare.

"Boss, why don't you go home for a while? I'll stay," Sal appealed, setting a discomfited hand on Linc's shoulder.

"Don't." Linc's gaze remained on the lifeless form in the hospital bed.

Sal shifted closer, squeezing his shoulder. "It's been two weeks. Go home, get a shower, change clothes and come back."

Linc buried his head in the stiff mattress, holding the motionless hand. "Go away," he growled.

Sal glanced at Serena's pale face and whispered, "Okay, boss."

Not long after, a nurse followed by a doctor entered, positioning themselves on each side. "Mr. Jefferson."

Linc gradually picked up his head, wet bloodshot eyes glaring at the intrusion.

"We have to take her for some tests now."

Linc stood and leaned over, kissing her temple, eyelids, cheeks, and lips. He whispered in her ear, "I'll be back," and pressed her limp hand to his lips before exiting.

A book in one hand and the other caressing Serena's, Linc read her favorite stories aloud for hours each day. His inflections deepened by his heartfelt tone, emphasizing each word with tender loving care.

The rapid knock had Linc looking up at the opening door.

"How is she?" Jax sat down on the opposite side, concern in his voice.

"The same." He indexed the page he just finished and set the novel on the bed.

Jax's gaze scanned Serena. "How you doing?"

Linc stroked her hand, staring at the wall without answering.

"Doc give you any updates?"

Linc whispered, "She needs time…" Closing his eyes he added, "to heal."

"Why don't you get out of here? You eat anything?"

No comment.

Jax sighed. "She'll need you strong when she wakes up." He stood. "Focus on that. Not the past."

Linc darted a scowl at Jax and roared, "I should have protected her. She wouldn't have come after us if I'd given her more information. Told her there wasn't anything to worry about," and then he directed an insistent wake-up gaze on Serena.

"Come on, man, listen to yourself…look at me," Jax insisted, using a stubborn, knock-sense-into-you attitude.

Linc did, his pointed stare shooting bullets.

"It was *Mylaynee*. They had each other's back from the get-go. No matter what you said or wanted it wouldn't have made a difference."

After the rant, Linc turned his weary eyes to the soundless body.

"I'll be back tomorrow." Jax jerked his chin toward the bed. "If you need anything…" the offer trailed behind him.

"We miss you, Serena. Paulette bought the movies you've been wanting to see. She said we can't watch them until you come home." Mylaynee shifted in the plastic chair and pulled Serena's motionless hand up to her cheek. "Best Buddies is having a dance in a few weeks. Robby said you'd save him a dance. That's all he talks about. They're waiting for you too, Serena."

She reached into her purse and set a bundled stack on the bed. "I brought cards from the nursing home. They all send their best wishes. Mrs. Wainwright's card is the funniest. It has two old ladies on the front with dentures in their hands. It says, 'We're speechless without you. Get well soon.' I couldn't stop laughing. There's more too." She read every one aloud.

"I'm going to put these on the counter, so when you wake up you'll see them. They miss you too.

"We went to the animal shelter the other day. Fallon wants a puppy so bad." She glanced at Linc. His eyes fixed to the place they'd been all along. "I wouldn't mind a kitten. You should see them. I bet if you woke up, Linc would let you have one."

She scooted the wobbly chair closer and squeezed the weightless hand tighter. "I read those books you gave me. I liked the one about the boxer who fell in love with his female trainer. Smokin' hot, girlfriend. Bet you I get the next one in the series first. I just bought the same e-reader you have too. You're already listed in the contacts. Gotta wake up so I can dive into that thousand-plus collection you have. I got a lot of catching up to do."

After a brief chuckle, she said, "We could start a 'Book Babes' club. With your paperbacks and e-books, you'd keep us reading for years. The girls would drool over your erotica for sure. We might never sleep."

She redirected her gaze across the bed at the lone man. "Linc brought the good ones. I think he has a secret fetish for your stash. I'm warning you, girl. He's gonna want *you* to read to him before bed." She watched him for a reaction. The immobile figure didn't flinch. His only movement, a thumb caressing Serena's hand and his eyes searching her face.

"Maybe I should bring coffee. You crave it so much, I bet the smell would wake you up. Serena, your man's losing weight. At least ten pounds. You wouldn't want him wasting away, would you?"

She placed her hand on his. "Linc…" squeezing it, "can I bring you something to eat?"

Without looking at her, he answered by shifting his bearded chin left then right.

She stood and kissed Serena's cold cheek. "I'll see you tomorrow," she whispered in her ear, "It's time, my dear friend…" On a choked sigh she pleaded, "Wake up. Linc's waiting for you, honey. He hasn't left your side. Needs *you,* sweetie. Please wake up for him, okay?" The fervent appeals trailed along with her overflowing tears.

She gave Linc an awkward one-arm hug. His face turned in the opposite direction, she couldn't see the moisture in his eyes or the tears dripping off his trembling chin.

Her departure and sentiments stirred the solemn being. He rose from his seat, and with gentle care, he enfolded Serena in his loving arms and whispered the wish engraved upon his heart and soul. The one envisioned at first sight, when her brilliant and magnificent light captured his enigmatic, tormented spirit.

Chapter Twenty-Six

Darkness and nothingness transformed to awareness—a familiar and favorite story, often read before bedtime, registered.

The maiden Madeline gathered berries in her apron-skirt, eating them along the way. Tired from the long walk, her legs dragged and kicked up dirt-filled dust that covered her cowhide shoes. A horse's snort brought her gaze upward from the log blocking her path.

Silver tassels braided in the mane covered its withers, extending to girth. Sure footed the white stallion stood at attention outside her straw hut. Unsure who the beauty belonged to, she hesitated with each step. Out of the corner of her eye, a blurry vision came into view. A Viking warrior in body armor stumbled toward her and collapsed at her feet...

"Fair Maiden, help me," he gasped...

A man's voice: poignant, summoning.

Pain and pressure diminished, replaced with warmth, emanating through my toes, legs, chest, and head—granting exodus. A delicate caress and strong grasp bid me to join in, infusing me with its intense presence and beckoning my mind and body—to rouse.

Consciousness came. Heedful to comply to fate's whispered call.

A vision emerged—a man with long black hair covering his massive shoulders and a scruffy beard lining his jaw, reciting the tale from a book in his lap. Mesmerized by his tone, I listened as he relayed the beauty of the love story—two strangers brought together—fate's affirmation.

Memories flickered, one flashback to the next, compelling me to respond. His thumb rubbing my hand was returned when I swiped mine across his knuckle, delivering a voluntary and hard-fought communication.

Blue, hazy eyes darted to mine. Book forgotten, Linc rose, gasping, "Serena." He captured my face in his hands and pressed his warm lips to my temple, eyelids, cheeks, and mouth. "You came back to me…" He drew in a ragged breath and announced, "I missed you. I…" He advanced once again, the kiss tender and full of devotion. He rested his temple on mine. "I've been waiting so long for you."

I wiggled my toes, shifted my legs, and squeezed my hands open and closed, loosening my limbs. "What happened?" My dry throat made the gruff plea burn in my mouth.

Instead of answering, he punched a button on the wall. When a reply came, Linc implored, "We need a doctor. She's awake."

The Fab Five swarmed into my hospital room and took over, giving Linc a much-needed reprieve. Their amped-up estrogen consuming the cramped space might've been a contributing factor too. Uncontained chit-chatter updated me on anything and everything I missed the past two weeks. The only break in conversation came when a loud knock demanded it.

An electrical charge of a different kind revved up the room when the stranger entered. Instead of focusing on his face like everyone else, my eyes got stuck on the shiny badge clipped to a belt on his low-riding jeans. "Miss Thomas," he called out, which brought my stare up to his whisky-brown eyes. Presented with a smorgasbord and too many options to choose from, his keen focus shifted from me to Fallon, Sage, and Paulette, devouring them at a leisurely pace. "Ladies, I don't believe we've met. I'm Detective Collins." His down-in-the-gutter gritty tone had the entire room swooning, pleasing the female crowd with an eye-scanning introduction that said, *I'd like your name and measurements.* When he got to Mylaynee, his visual appetite feasted as if capsized on a deserted island without an ounce of nourishment. "Miss Johanson, nice to see you again."

Interesting.

Mylaynee, protector of all and guardian angel, swooped in, blocking my view.

I shifted around her blockade, from one side to the other, watching the detective amble in a cocky hip swagger from one to the next, greeting each of them with another visual body search and unhurried handshake.

Instead of following suit, Mylaynee crossed her arms and repositioned her body in my direct line of sight, again. "This isn't a good time," the mother bear growled with hands clenched at her elbows, digging two-inch nails into her flesh. "You got my report, Jax and Linc too. She can't tell you anything more than we did."

He propped an elbow in one hand and stroked the stubble at the corner of his mouth, drawing attention to his supple lips and every word that came out of them. "That may be, but she's the injured party and I need to question her."

Mylaynee opened her mouth to reply, but he took a step and leaned over her, considering me. All cockiness and swagger aside, he asked with kindness and a sympathetic assessment, "Miss Thomas, I put it off as long as I could. Your doctor gave the okay since you've been up and walking around the past five days. Could we talk a few minutes?"

Linc came barreling through the door, redirecting everyone's attention, including the detective's. Faster than I'd ever seen them move before, a mass round of hugs and goodbyes took place, leaving three behind.

"Linc, it's good to see you under better circumstances." The officer's informal greeting had me swiping glances between them.

In a protective stance, hand-in-hand at my side, Linc squeezed my palm and reprimanded the cop. "You should've called me."

"Want to let me do my job?" He jerked his chin toward Linc, giving as good as he got. "I'll let you stay if you keep your cool. Can you do that?"

"Fuck you, Reese." Shocked by his sharp quip, I yanked on his hand. He glanced down, and I shook my head, trying to get him shut up. Regardless of whether they knew each other or not, I didn't want him arrested.

Instead the detective laughed. "Yeah, that's what I thought. Miss Thomas, what do you say?"

"Serena, you don't have to do this now."

Ping-ponging between these two was getting on my nerves. "I'm good." I turned onto my side to address the visitor head on, adjusting my body higher to relieve some of the numbness in my legs. "Let's get this over with."

He nodded, pulled out a notepad, and began the interrogation.

At every prompt Linc tensed and with each reply he squeezed my hand, a supportive gesture and a constant reminder of his presence. Like I could forget, since he refused to remain silent, trying my patience, and if the pinched lips and perturbed glares the detective shot him were any indication, I'd say he felt the same.

Most details of that night were fuzzy, so I couldn't relay much. According to Mylaynee and verified during questioning, Rick still hadn't been caught. The police weren't giving up and from what little Linc shared with me earlier, neither was Jax. The events could've been a lot worse. I was grateful Mylaynee hadn't been hurt. From the account she provided, Rick had her bound and gagged in the warehouse but unharmed. On the way to the hospital, Jax got a security team to scour the area they had to rush out of, because of me. When I thought about the disastrous result and the additional problems my presence could have cost, I felt like shooting me too. If I had caused anyone to be injured other than myself, I don't know how I would have lived with it. My "new" family meant a great deal to me, and I wouldn't want anything to happen to them.

Later, when it was just the two of us, Linc climbed into bed, hauled me onto his lap and read to me. Instead of a novel, he recited in a mellow, affecting tone classic poetry from an anthology that had a worn and well-loved cover. The inscription on the first page was written by a devoted mother to her cherished son.

Lincoln,
My soul's first embrace, cradled you with tender loving care.
My heart entwined to yours, enlivened from beat one.
My love transcends eternity, a guiding star enlightening the darkness.
May your soul nurture.
May your heart treasure.
May your love inspire.

My fingers traced each phrase, admiring the woman, and the adoration expressed, wishing I could have met her. Cuddled to his side, my head nestled on his shoulder, he recited each poem with his lips pressed to my temple. Every one of his fortifying breaths and inspirational stanzas revitalized my spirit, while his determined stronghold worshipped, cherished, and enlivened. Just as his mother had wished.

Chapter Twenty-Seven

Even though I had been in good shape before my incident, the doctors said it could take months for me to rebound. A cerebral contusion and blood loss sent my system in a spiral, resulting in minimal consciousness the entire time I'd been there. Either a dream or reality, I wasn't sure which, arriving at the hospital and afterward became a blur. Being "out of it" for two weeks resulted in bouts of overwhelming fatigue and stilted movements. Headaches and memory loss, considered "normal," occurred from the moment I woke up. For some reason, selective bits and pieces of the shooting and surrounding events remain lost, and might never return. Maybe the brain knew best. At least I hadn't forgotten the most important people. Linc, Mylaynee, and the rest of the group encouraged me to get up and move, so I could get out of the rehab center quicker. Not that I wanted to stay anyway.

Although painful, the puckered and scarring skin from the wound under my right breast looked better each day. My collapsed lung took a while to heal, but it improved too. Orders included a physical therapist to build strength and target conditioning. My movements at first resembled a ninety-year-old behind a walker, but with light weights incorporated in the sessions, I graduated to a dawdling amble. Luckily, the overall prognosis had been positive and the residual effects few. Careful monitoring and every possible test ran at least twice, the doctors discharged me three weeks later.

In typical Fab Five style, the girls hosted a private gathering in the lounge a few days after I returned. I told them not to, especially after what I put them through, but they didn't listen. As close to a home as I had, this place and each person had come to mean a great deal to me. And Linc, although he had stuck with me through each excruciating moment, took the greatest hit. His constant doting, questions about how I felt, and worry etched into his cautious moves made me heartsick. The parallels between his sister and my unfortunate event put him on edge. He watched me constantly for any little twinge or residual pain. If the tables were turned, and he'd been injured, I would've been inconsolable. After everything he'd gone through, I could understand his concern.

No reservations remaining, I realized my purpose here was destined from the start. He needed me, and I knew there wasn't another man alive who would treasure me or enliven my spirit more. His unending support and the strength he exhibited before and after this ordeal proved his commitment to me. Perhaps a person's name dictated character and worth after all. Mr. Lincoln Jefferson possessed loyalty, honor, and compassion. Characteristics any woman would be proud to have in the man she loved.

Zoning out as various discussions carried on around me, the first person to pull me back into a conversation had been the one who contributed to my setback.

"You're looking well, Serena." Jax plopped into the empty chair next to me, propped an ankle across his knee, and flung an arm around the back of my chair. Mr. Casual instead of Mr. Gigolo still annoyed the heck out of me.

"I'm fine, thanks." I launched my best blasé reply, catching his smirk out of the corner of my eye and diverting my glance around the room at everyone else but him. Rude I know, but he rubbed me the wrong way.

"Good, if you need anything, let me know." Ugh! The emphasis he placed on "anything" sent chills up my spine. Mylaynee's guttural giggle had me shooting her an annoyed scowl. She shook her head and twirled her finger in a cuckoo motion at her temple and mouthed, "Fuckin' with you." Jax snatched her by the neck and gave her a noogie.

She slapped his arm away and jerked back in her seat, flicking her mussed hair into place. "Stop messin' with her already. Haven't you done enough?"

In slow motion, he turned to me, smiles all gone. His pained stare pierced my heart. "I never told you how sorry I am." His raspy apology came across as the most sincere emotion I'd ever seen from him. If I learned one thing from this entire experience, life was too short. I didn't want to spend it angry or resentful.

My hand placed on top of his, I absolved him of any guilt. "It wasn't your fault."

"Thanks, but I'll get him."

"Please don't. Let the police handle it." Linc set a hand on my shoulder, butting into the conversation. "He's not going to do anything, Serena. You don't need to worry about it, okay? Jax, let it go." His clipped directive got a stiff nodded reply.

Impeccable timing as always, B.B. snuck up to Linc's side, petting his arm from shoulder to wrist. "Could I talk to you a minute?"

Oh, hell to the no, this wasn't happening today. Before I could tell her off, Linc interceded. "What's the problem?"

"Can we go to your office?"

Yeah, I knew what she wanted.

"Is it business?"

My raised brows couldn't be missed by anybody at the table. Not a dunce, I couldn't figure out why he gave her the time of day. Talk about head games, she mastered the class and probably did it on her knees.

"Uh, no. It's important though."

Bullshit, wench.

He glanced at me then back to her. "Not now."

How about never?

When she made her next move, gliding her hand across his chest, I leapt out of my chair, quicker than I'd moved in the last month, and clamped down on her wrist. "Don't. Touch. Him."

She quirked a brow at me and glanced around the table, shouting louder than a foghorn. "Or what, Sadrena?" She yanked, trying to free her arm from my iron grip, but I countered by bending her hand at a nearly ninety-degree angle, almost snapping it. Her whimper, a death-defying scream in the silent room.

"I know your secret." Panic pinched her brow and sweat dotted her forehead. "You've been telling tall tales, B.B." Eye to eye, nose to nose, and shedding all moral dignity, I let it all hang out. "Linc didn't sleep with you. And he *never* will." I tossed her arm aside and returned to my man. His arm wound around my hip, pulling me flush to his side.

B.B. stormed out faster than a tornado, tossing out expletives and flinging the door shut. Her trailing squeals echoed in the room after she left.

Adrenaline rush over, I winced from the pain pinching my ribs. Winded from the overexertion, I clutched the chair and sat back down, slow and unsteady. Jax and Mylaynee smirked at each other. Sal, not one for many words, said, "That otta do it." Fallon, Paulette, and Sage agreed with a resounding, "Yep," "About time," and "You go, girl." All the other employees joined too, eager to get their two cents in.

Linc came up behind me, squeezing my shoulders. "Okay?" I leaned my head against his arm and looked up, frowning and feeling bad about handling the situation that way, even if it had been long overdue. He slid onto my chair, propping me on his lap. "Defending my honor, huh? Watch out, no one better mess with me. I have my own bodyguard now." His smart-alecky comment got him a pinch to his stomach, and I ground my knuckles in for good measure, making sure he felt every bit of it. Merriment filled the lounge as my exaggerated movements made it apparent to everyone what I'd done.

Mylaynee jumped out of her seat, clapping three times. "Okay, time for cake. We got chocolate, vanilla, and Serena's favorite, white almond. Speak up now or forever hold your peace," she shouted. Everyone cheered and yelled orders one after another. The sugar junkies argued over who wanted what piece and the positive mood returned. An entire sheet cake and four gallons of ice cream devoured, no one could be anything but stuffed with blissful happiness.

Chapter Twenty-Eight

I heard voices but couldn't figure out what they said. Their hushed mumbles grew louder. Curious, I got out of bed and threw on a robe, sneaking down the hall toward Linc's living room. Two distinct males arguing became clearer when I reached the entryway.

Shoot, not again.

I spun around, but the next declaration brought my silent footsteps to a halt.

"You going to propose?"

Dammit, Jax, do you ever shut up!

"Don't you have an appointment to get to?"

Yeah, B.B.'s waiting to sink her fangs and venom breath into you now that Linc isn't up for grabs.

"After everything that's happened, it's not on your mind?"

"I'm not talking to you about it."

"Why not?"

"Back the fuck off. You've been riding my ass since you got here."

"Hmm…"

"What?"

"I'll drop it, man." Jax's snickers followed his brisk response.

"Say it then. Stop being a dick."

"Alright. It's time to move on. Get the hell out of here, give Serena a home. I'll make you an offer you can't refuse. Sell me the business."

"Stop."

"Why? You stubborn fuck. You still don't see what's right in front of you, do you? Come on man, you want this the rest of your life? It's been *years*, stop punishing yourself."

"Get out."

"Linc—"

"Now! Or I'll throw you the fuck out."

The door slammed just as the outburst ended.

Shit.

Hunched over with his head buried in his hands, Linc's over-boiling temper and the tension lining his stiff back pressurized the atmosphere and turned the air in the room to suffocating.

I placed a gentle hand on his shoulder, and he jerked up, anger visible on his flushed face. "Uh...um..." My throat clogged from the pain radiating off him.

"How much did you hear?"

Seated next to him, I positioned my hand on his knee, squeezing it. "Enough."

He cupped my cheek, and his intense stare held me in place, keeping me silent. "Right now, all that matters is your health. Let's get you better. Everything else can wait."

Hello? He couldn't be serious. "Let's talk now."

He sucked in a deep breath and exhaled real slow, inspecting my face, but I didn't know for what. "Tell me what you want."

It took me a while to answer. My mind formulating the right words and calculating the pros and cons of venturing into the unknown. "We've both lost a lot. Even though it was just Gram and me, I never felt lonely with her at my side. I'd like to have a family and home someday. And I want that for *you* too."

He wandered to the windows, a blank stare cast out to the foggy harbor. Quiet a long time, he redirected his aim at me. A softness unlike any I'd ever seen on his face before replaced his heated one. "You can have it." Then the rigid lines on his forehead returned as he divulged, "But I can't..." Closing his eyes, he didn't bother finishing, pure agony evident in his clenched fists and pinched mouth.

My heart dropped and my body reacted to his, stiffening with dread. Jax's speech came to me at that moment: "Stop punishing yourself."

Why didn't it register before?

No freaking way. I would not let this wonderful, caring man spend one more second torturing himself. Wrapping my arms around him, I placed my head on his back and listened to the steady, powerful beat. My heart breaking for a man determined to be a martyr.

Please, I need to help him. What could I say?

"Linc, have you told your sister how you feel?"

He twisted around, grabbed my shoulders and extended his long arms full length, making the gap between us enormous.

The earlier vehemence in his voice returned. "What are you talking about?"

Not sure where the hell that spouted from, I stood there dumbstruck and mute. His face turned redder the longer I stayed silent. The negative vibes coming off him zinged through every cell in my body, pounding in my head and making me woozy.

I had no right. *Why the hell did I say that?*

Control and patience gone, he grabbed my upper arms and shook me. "How dare you," he snapped.

The jolt must have rattled my brain because my mouth opened, sealing my fate. "She wouldn't want you blaming yourself." My arms flung out wide as I spoke, encompassing the room, but literally meant the business and what he thought he deserved.

"You don't know what the hell you're talking about. You didn't know my sister, you didn't see her beaten, on her death bed. You haven't spent *years* wishing she got better. Where the fuck do you get off bringing her into this?"

Fury and encompassing pain lightened my head and blurred my vision.

Then—nothing.

Beep. Beep. Beep.

Hands tugged at me as pain radiated everywhere. The ringing in my ears blocked out any other sound.

Ew. *What's that smell?*

My eyes shot open as the circulation in my arm and pulse cut off.

A man in a blue medic uniform knelt beside me, blood pressure cuff pumped to full capacity. A flickering beam flashed into my eyes, making me pinch them closed.

What the heck?

I opened them and examined the room. Linc and Mylaynee hovered at my feet. On my other side, another medic pushed a needle in my arm, making me wince at the sudden jab.

Linc came around the side and knelt at the top of my head, brushing my hair to the side and off my forehead. "I'm so sorry, please forgive me."

Not having a clue, I concentrated on his pale face and tried to remember what happened.

"Please," he begged, pressing his lips to my temple.

Blood pressure cuff off, I lifted my free hand up to his cheek, my palm covering the tears cascading down them. "It's okay."

Before I could say anything else, they hoisted me onto a stretcher. Mylaynee clasped my hand in hers, rushing alongside and reassuring. "Don't worry. They just have to check you out."

I grabbed Linc's hand and gazed up with a pleading expression, willing him not to leave me.

In some reciprocal, unspoken exchange, I knew he wouldn't—ever.

Somehow doctors and nurses thought it necessary to poke and prod, when all I wanted was to be left alone. They performed their duties with proficiency, but my grumbles and impatience didn't help me get out of there any faster. I prayed to never step foot in a hospital again. After several rounds of tests, all coming back clear, I returned in time to go to bed. Daylight gone and almost ten o'clock, fatigue had set in, even though I hadn't done more than get wheeled from one room to another. Swaddled in a comforter, Linc spooning behind me, I couldn't keep my eyes open.

"What can I get you?"

Geez, would I ever get any peace? On a yawn I murmured, "I'm good." I kicked the heavy blanket to the side, and Linc pulled it the rest of the way down, leaving a single sheet covering my waist. He picked up my hand, kissing it tenderly. "I'm sorry, Serena."

He'd said it least a hundred times in the ambulance, at the hospital, and on the way home. Knowing I wouldn't be able to fall asleep with him beating himself up anymore, I turned around and wrapped my arms around his waist. "You had every right to be angry." I tilted his face down, bringing him almost nose to nose, and spoke with utter determination. "This place does *not* define you, Linc. You deserve to have everything your heart desires. I brought up your sister because her tragedy should have one and only one significance."

I placed a cherished kiss on his lips and cast my heartfelt wish. "Live *for* her, not *because* of her."

His blue eyes lightened, so pastel they looked fluorescent. I watched an interchange of expressions from thoughtful to acceptance to emboldened take hold, washing a decade of pain and tumult off him.

His pupils transformed to pinpricks, and he roamed my face in slow motion. He repeated the same action with his fingertips, skimming from my temple, to cheeks, and down to my chin. *Oh, Linc.* He did the same thing the first day we met.

He flashed me that crooked, dimpled smile, and slid his thumb in a tender swipe across my lower lip, whispering, "My serenity. I love you, Serena."

THE END

Linc & Serena's story is continued in SERENITY.
Available 2015.

Dear Readers,

Thank you for reading INTENSITY. If you enjoyed it, I would appreciate a shout out.

Review it: Please consider writing a review, either at the retailer site where you purchased INTENSITY, or on your blog. If you post a review, let me know. I read a lot too, write reviews on occasion, but not spoilers. Please do me a favor, preserve the story. When I read reviews I like to be teased, but I don't want to be told everything. That's why I rarely read movie descriptions and often choose books by covers and teasers. I love surprises, especially good ones.

Recommend it: Know other romance readers? Please let them know about INTENSITY. Recommend it to friends, family, book clubs, and others via social media. I'm always looking for the next great read too. Do you have a suggestion? Let me know about it.

Visit my website: www.cckoen.com. Access the blog page and read my book recommendations. I post once a month and only my Fab Favs (fabulous favorites) make it.

Upcoming projects: SERENITY release 2015. This story picks up where INTENSITY left you. Want to know what happens with Serena & Linc? It's not over yet. Visit my website www.cckoen.com for updates and excerpts. There are tons of INTENSITY goodies there too. Check them out. Have you seen the INTENSITY book trailer yet? Warning: It's smokin' hot. It's on the website along with a playlist and in-depth character info.

Curious about other INTENSITY characters?
Mylaynee's story will be available in 2016. You won't believe

how she ended up at the lounge. Love mystery and suspense? There will be plenty in her book: (untitled).

Chit-chat w/me:

Romance blog: authorcckoen.com

Addicted to romance? I am! Join me at the romance blog where I post a discussion topic each month. Comment on book crushes and real-life love stories. Come by to share or just hang out a while.

Facebook: www.facebook.com/cckoenbooks

Twitter: http://twitter.com/authorcckoen @authorcckoen

Goodreads: www.goodreads.com/authorcckoen

I'm new to social media. Bear with me as I navigate through these beasts and learn via crash courses. Ugh!

Create:

Are you a techie? Do you have a great speaking voice? INTENSITY fan? Help me build a fan page for my website. Would you like to contribute? Here's how:

1. Create audio excerpts from INTENSITY.
2. Create a video about INTENSITY.
3. Create a dream cast.
4. Create teasers.

Send it to me via my website contact page, FB, Twitter, or Pinterest.

Author Bio

I grew up in a culturally rich, bilingual home which included unique holiday celebrations and wonderful ethnic foods passed down through generations. My favorites are the sweets of course.

An educator for over twenty years, my passion includes teaching, reading, and writing. An avid reader who enjoys romance, mystery, and suspense, my stories will never be what you expect. Teacher by day, romance writer at night produce an active imagination I share with each of you.

Join me on this journey…

Dream big dreams—they're always in reach, just grab on and enjoy the ride.

Acknowledgements

C.B.—You've been with me from the beginning: a mentor, cheerleader, psychologist, social media tutor, and so much more. You took me under your wing at WCES and haven't stopped since. Thank you for the constant support and inspiration. Your friendship means the world to me.

K.T.—Certain people come into your life for very specific reasons. From day one, we were not only colleagues, but best friends. Thank you for always listening, the prayers and guidance, and for putting up with the "sass" I dish out too often. The nickname you gave me fits so well.

Bloggers—The Book Enthusiast, Book Plug Promotions, HEA Bookshelf, Reading Addiction VBT, RomCon Blogs, Tasty Book Tours, Truly Schmexy Girl/PR, XPresso Book Tours, Author Cate Masters, InkslingerPR, and InD'tale. Thank you for the support and guidance throughout the daunting marketing process. My questions were mundane, but you answered and encouraged every time. Without the hard work all of you do, authors would have a hard time connecting with readers. From one avid reader to another, thanks for helping us find the next great read!

Beta Readers—Amazing writers and readers, my heartfelt thanks to the many Scrib members who provided thorough critiques. I'm in awe of your stories, poetry, and literary genius. Your thoughtful insights pushed me to be a better writer and the constant encouragement helped me get through the zany writing process. A wonderful group of experts and professionals who know what it takes to write a great story. Thank you!

D.P. Lyle, M.D.—You are proof of the power of social media. I never would have found out about Crime & Scene Radio or the consulting service you provide for authors if it hadn't been for a recommendation I received via Twitter. Thank you for your insight and perspective about guns and resulting injuries.

E. Pepper, M.D.—My family practice doctor, thank you for taking time out of your very busy schedule to make sure all my questions were answered. You rock!

H.A. Puttgen, M.D.—YOU ARE AMAZING! Whether you drew the short straw or not, I appreciate the nearly hour-long phone conference and multiple emails you answered. I wasn't sure anyone would respond to my requests for assistance, but you did. You explained medical terminology and critical care methods with such clarity that I actually understood it. I don't know if you'll ever read this book, but if you do, I hope I did you proud.